McGuire, Manhunter

Manhunter Jim McGuire hung up his gun and settled in White Ridge aiming to live a quiet life, but his past profession soon called him back. His young charge Billy Jameson was wrongly accused of murder and the only way to save him from the gallows was to take on an assignment from the corrupt Mayor Jake Nixon.

But finding the on-the-run thief Barney Dale wasn't as straightforward as it seemed. Barney was the only witness to a murder committed by Nixon and unbeknown to Jim, the mayor has hired ruthless guns to ensure that as soon as he finds Barney both of their lives will be cut short.

With the manhunter becoming the hunted man, can Jim defeat the many guns Nixon has lined up against him?

By the same author

Ambush in Dust Creek
Silver Gulch Feud
Blood Gold
Golden Sundown
Clearwater Justice
Hellfire
Escape from Fort Benton
Return to Black Rock
The Man They Couldn't Hang
Last Stage to Lonesome

McGuire, Manhunter

Scott Connor

A Black Horse Western

ROBERT HALE · LONDON

© Scott Connor 2009
First published in Great Britain 2009

ISBN 978-0-7090-8735-9

Robert Hale Limited
Clerkenwell House
Clerkenwell Green
London EC1R 0HT

www.halebooks.com

Typeset by
Derek Doyle & Associates, Shaw Heath
Printed and bound in Great Britain by
CPI Antony Rowe, Chippenham and Eastbourne

CHAPTER 1

'The kid's gone loco,' Orson Brown said, slamming his fist on the bar.

Jim McGuire winced. He'd dreaded hearing news of this kind all week.

'I'll speak to him,' he said, then pushed the whiskey bottle along the bar as an added encouragement to Orson to listen to his plea.

Orson snorted, but the bottle was just too tempting, so he poured himself a glass, then leaned on the bar beside Jim.

'There's no point,' he said, his tone becoming more reasonable. 'Billy's not cut out to work for a newspaper. He'll have to go elsewhere.'

The two men looked at each other, both avoiding mentioning the obvious point that for the last six months Jim had tried to find work for Billy in just about every possible place in White Ridge. Nothing had worked out. Billy wasn't cut out to work in Chester Heart's mercantile, or the saloon, or the hotel. Even shovelling manure in the stables seemed to be an activity he found too taxing.

'What was the problem this time?'

'He's lazy and ornery,' Orson said, giving a rueful smile. 'Newspapers require dedication, but he's been late every day. So I punished him by telling him he's *worked* for a week for nothing, but he got so angry I reckoned he might smash up the place and throw me through the window.'

Orson gulped his drink, then raised his eyebrows, inviting a response.

'I'm sorry, and I can't offer much in the way of inducement.' Jim topped up Orson's glass. 'But if you change your mind, I'll do everything I can do to make sure he's on time and works hard.'

Orson sighed. 'I know it's hard for you, Jim, and I don't blame you for Billy's actions. Bringing up a kid who ain't your own can't be easy.'

'It ain't,' Jim said, letting his voice become wistful. 'Billy's father was a good friend and I promised him before he died that I'd give his boy a good start in life. That's all I'm trying to do.'

Jim only called upon this form of emotional blackmail when he was desperate. So far he'd used this tale on five different employers and each time it'd worked, but only the once.

Orson sipped his drink while shaking his head, but, with Jim smiling at him, he gave a reluctant nod.

'All right. He'll get that second chance, provided he's on time tomorrow and provided he apologizes, then shows some enthusiasm.'

Jim patted Orson's back and moved to refill his

6

glass, but he noticed that further down the bar Chester Heart was listening to their conversation. So before he had a chance to join them and relate some tales of the three traumatic days Billy had worked for him, Jim ushered Orson outside.

On the boardwalk Orson urged Jim to stay there for now to avoid inflaming the situation, then headed across the road to the newspaper office. Jim watched him leave, then cast his gaze down the road, already resigned to this assignment not working out and wondering where else he could try to get permanent employment for his unruly charge.

It wasn't that Billy was bad: he was just young and he didn't seem prepared to do any work at all. Maybe if he was his real father, Jim mused not for the first time, he'd know what to say to get through to him.

But the wise words of his kin was something Billy would never receive again and so, as he had done the previous times, Jim told himself that it was just a matter of letting Billy work through his problems. For his part, he'd continue to support him until he found work that suited him and then. . . .

A gunshot tore out, the sound muffled.

The few people out on the road stopped in their tracks, ducking and cringing while looking around for where the shot had come from. It had been some time since Jim had last drawn his own gun, so he merely lowered his hand towards his holster while looking around.

Then he saw that several people were looking towards the newspaper office, torn between rushing to investigate and scurrying away. Jim had no such qualms. He broke into a run and reached the office door before anyone else had stepped up on to the boardwalk; then he threw open the door.

Inside Orson Brown lay on his back clutching his chest, blood oozing through his fingers. Billy was on one knee beside him, shock contorting his young face. That shock deepened when Orson uttered a choked-off gasp, then arched his back and flopped down to lie still. Billy looked up at Jim.

'It wasn't me,' he murmured.

Jim looked around the office, seeing nobody else inside, but his gaze fell on the open and swinging back door.

'I know. Who did do it?'

'I don't know. One moment he was shouting at me, and then. . . .' Billy uttered a sob and lowered his head as the horror of the situation finally took control of his emotions.

Jim would have consoled him but the open door at the back and his old instincts were beckoning him.

'I'll deal with it,' he said. He moved off, but he had taken only one step towards the door when the loud but shaking voice of Sheriff George Price spoke up from the door behind him.

'Reach or die!'

Jim stomped to a halt, then slowly turned with his hands raised slightly.

'Every second we waste,' he said, 'gives whoever did this another second to get away.'

'Wrong. I'm looking at that man right now.'

Jim glanced at Billy. Blood coated the young lad's hands and he was hunched over the body. He had to admit that even for a lawman who was as incompetent as Price was, this did appear to be a clear-cut situation, and one which was bad for Billy.

'He didn't do this. He doesn't even wear a gun.'

'He does. Look! He's going to shoot again.' Price's eyes opened wider as behind him on the boardwalk people began muttering and peering around him to see what was happening inside.

Billy wasn't holding the gun that Price reckoned he was holding, but there was a simpler explanation for Price's confusion. It was common knowledge that since the sheriff had given up the whiskey his judgement had become poor. Worse, he hadn't been particularly competent when he had been drinking, and in his darting eyes Jim could see his customary indecision. A wrong move from anyone could panic him into pulling the trigger.

Jim put on a calm expression he didn't feel and took a long pace towards Price to put himself between the lawman and Billy.

'Sure. Do your duty, Sheriff, and you'll see this situation ain't what it seems.'

Jim's closeness made Price gulp before he firmed his gun hand.

'Then stand aside and let me arrest Billy before he shoots up anyone else.'

Jim saw the sudden and rare flash of determination in Price's eyes. So he moved as if to step aside, but then swung round and with lightning reflexes

9

hammered a powerful uppercut into Price's jaw that sent him spinning away to thud into the wall.

With his back against the wall Price slid downwards until he came to a halt in a sitting position. He shook himself, but by the time he'd gathered what passed for his senses, Jim had moved in and taken his gun.

He held the weapon high along with his own so that the townsfolk looking in through the door weren't alarmed.

'Sorry I had to do that, but I couldn't risk you shooting Billy. He's an innocent. . . .' Jim trailed off when he saw the surprise in Price's eyes, his hand rising to point past him.

Jim swirled round, then frowned. Aside from them and the body of Orson Brown the office was otherwise deserted.

Billy had run.

CHAPTER 2

The back door of the newspaper office had been boarded up.

Jim kicked the door but the boards held firm, not that going inside again would help him. Last week he'd examined the whole office in his search for clues without success.

He turned to place his back to the door and looked around, trying to picture in which direction Orson's murderer would have fled so that he would disappear from view quickly. But he failed to come up with any new ideas that he hadn't considered already.

Ten days had passed since Orson Brown's death and so far there was only one suspect: Jim's young charge Billy Jameson.

Hector Pike, one of Mayor Nixon's personal body-guards, and Deputy Carter had found Billy within an hour of his running from the scene of the murder. His behaviour both before and after the death, along with Sheriff Price's belief that Billy had been kneeling over Orson's body holding a gun, was all the evidence they

11

had on him. But it would probably be enough.

Jim was the only other person to have a clear view of what had happened. He knew that Billy didn't carry a gun and he hadn't seen one in his hand, but his admittedly biased word against the sheriff's might not convince a court of Billy's innocence. So Jim had investigated on his own, figuring that bringing the real murderer to justice was the best way to get Billy freed.

But every avenue he'd explored had ended in failure. Orson Brown just didn't have any enemies. Now all that was stopping Billy's trial from going ahead was the distraction of the forthcoming elections for the new mayor. Accordingly, out on the main road the current incumbent, Mayor Jake Nixon, the man most likely to get elected, was making a speech punctuated with subdued cheers from the watching townsfolk.

Keeping his mind blank to avoid listening to the droning platitudes Jim ran his gaze along the backs of the buildings, then flinched. A face was looking at him from an alley. Then it disappeared from view when the person noted his interest.

Intrigued, Jim hurried to the alley. He slowed a few paces away and turned the corner to find he was facing Sheriff Price, standing with his back against the wall.

'You're watching me,' Jim said in a matter-of-fact manner, then cast his mind back over the last few days, 'again.'

'Sure am,' Price murmured, looking at his feet. 'I'm wondering what you're doing.'

'I'm trying to work out who killed Orson Brown.'

'That's my job.'

'Then do it!' Jim muttered and advanced a pace on Price, making him slink backwards for a few paces down the alley.

'Don't have to. I already know who did it.'

'You can't think you have enough to convict Billy, surely.'

'Mayor Nixon reckons so.'

Jim blew out his cheeks in exasperation, now understanding Price's lack of enthusiasm for carrying out the duties for which he had been appointed. Nothing happened in White Ridge without Mayor Nixon's approval, and that included the provision of justice.

'So Nixon told you to stop investigating, did he? Told you that Billy fitted the crime and you should look no further?'

'Yeah,' Price murmured, his voice barely audible.

Jim took another pace towards Price, his hand rising to bat away a fly, but Price mistook the hand movement for an aggressive act. While backing away he raised his arms to ward off a blow, but his feet became entangled and he tripped, then fell to the ground.

'Price,' Jim said, looking down at the lawman lying in an undignified heap, 'you're not only a sad excuse for a lawman, you're a sad excuse for a man.'

With that comment Jim stepped over Price's legs and headed down the alley.

When he came out on the main road Nixon was still standing on the podium in front of his office and inflicting a speech on the menfolk gathered in the road. As Jim now knew that to help Billy he would have to tackle Nixon first, he listened to his speech, aiming to speak to him when it ended.

The first words he heard made him grind his teeth.

'I stand for justice,' Nixon announced in a clear and authoritative voice. 'If re-elected my first action will be to ensure that the murderous piece of scum who killed my good friend Orson Brown gets the hanging he deserves.'

Nixon paused to cast a slow look around the crowd. Everyone slowly picked up on his cue that they needed to applaud, and the enthusiastic nature of that applause irritated Jim even more than he had been already. When he'd spoken to people everyone had appeared sympathetic to Billy's plight and had agreed that he wasn't a killer.

'And so I have no doubt,' Nixon continued, 'you will elect me in the forthcoming battle between myself and the other worthy candidates.'

Nixon gestured to the three men standing beside the podium. The deadline for announcing an interest in standing for election was sundown the following day, but Jim gathered from the gesture that these men had already stated they would stand. Of the three of them the businessman, Sherman Donner, stood straight-backed and confident, whereas the owners of the two biggest mercantiles in town, Chester Heart and Ronald Malone were standing hunched and unenthusiastic.

'But whoever you support I hope everyone will take part in the democratic principles that have made this

14

country great, and may the best man for the job win through.' Nixon bestowed a wide smile and a knowing wink upon a man on the front row. 'As long as that man is me.'

Everyone but the other candidates uttered an appreciative chuckle after which the crowd started to disperse and return to going about their business. Nixon shook hands with the other three candidates and had a brief word with each. Chester and Ronald weren't enthusiastic about talking with him and so, as soon as they could, they hurried away towards the saloon. Sherman, however, was keen to discuss something.

While they talked Jim made his way over to the podium but before he reached it Nixon broke away from Sherman, the flash of anger in both men's eyes obvious even from some distance away. Sherman advanced a pace, but Hector Pike and Mitch Hyde, Nixon's increasingly obvious main bodyguards, stepped in. One cold look from them made Sherman step back and desist from trying to continue whatever disagreement had been taking place.

By the time Jim reached the podium Nixon was shaking hands with well-wishers, but after a whispered word in the ear from his principal aide Walter Fenton, he moved away before everyone had been favoured with a handshake. He slipped into his office with a last cheery wave, closely followed by the hired guns.

'Is Nixon free?' Jim called out through the dispersing crowd to Walter.

'He ain't,' Walter said, standing before the door.

'Then when can I see him?'

'You saw him make a speech. That's all the seeing *you* will get this week.' Walter laughed. 'But I'm sure he'll be free after the trial.'

With a narrowing of his eyes Jim acknowledged he'd heard the emphasis Walter had put into his reply, but that didn't stop Walter from following Nixon into the office. Jim didn't follow him in, figuring that with Nixon devoting the next week to campaigning, other chances would come his way soon enough.

He was about to leave and return to the back of the newspaper office when his attention was drawn again to the podium. A dozen or so people were still around, each man being slow to disperse as he enjoyed the opportunity to chat, and so, on a whim, Jim mounted the podium. His unexpected action gathered immediate interest.

'What you doing up there, Jim?' one man asked, smiling. 'You making a speech too?'

'You're right that I ain't a man for no fancy speech-making,' Jim said, then cleared his throat, 'but as everyone else has made one, perhaps I should too. So, what Nixon said about Billy Jameson was rot. Billy ain't no angel but he ain't no murderer either.'

'He shot Orson Brown,' the nearest man said. 'Sheriff Price saw him do it.'

'That rumour sure spread quickly and that's why I'm here, putting the record straight. Price reckoned Billy had a gun, but he didn't see him fire it, and I didn't see no gun at all. I can't prove that and Price can't prove his claim, so you'll have to decide whether you believe my word or his.'

'Ah,' the man said, lowering his head, the comment going on to gather a few encouraging grunts from the other watching men.

'And that's the problem with White Ridge,' Jim said, slapping his fist into his palm as he warmed to the task. 'Mayor Nixon controls everything. His version of the law is the only one allowed and it stinks. Sheriff Price is again the only man standing for sheriff because only he could accept being ordered around by Nixon. Yeah, the town's peaceful, but only for those people who agree with our mayor.'

Jim paused when the people who had been nodding before started to mutter that they disagreed with this. He thought through what he'd said and realized he'd veered away from his original intent. So, before he lost whatever support he'd gained, he decided to finish off.

'So look for options other than voting for a ticket of Nixon and Price. A young man's life is at stake and if you support their version of justice you'll have Billy's blood on your hands when I find out who really killed Orson Brown.'

With a last firm glare at the gathered men, Jim stepped down from the podium. Silence greeted him, although he judged it to be a thoughtful rather than a disapproving silence. He wended his way through the people, trying to catch anyone's eye. Only Sherman Donner looked his way and gave him a nod of support and a silent handclap.

As he walked away, he felt relieved that he'd spoken

17

his mind. For the last ten days his frustration had grown but the speech had helped to calm him down and perhaps suggest a possible way forward. With that in mind, he reckoned the days ahead would be sure to present him with more opportunities to attack Nixon, until the mayor agreed to speak with him.

Accordingly, when he reached the alley to go round behind the newspaper office he looked back. His gaze rose from the podium and the dispersing people to take in the mayor's office and there in the upstairs window, Mayor Nixon was watching him.

As ever, Pike and Hyde were flanking him, both hired guns standing with their arms dangling and their hands resting against their holsters as they watched his every move.

CHAPTER 3

'I'm not standing for mayor,' Ronald Malone said, drawing his horse to a halt before the two riders. 'I've left town and I ain't ever coming back.'

Hyde snorted while Pike smirked. Neither men moved aside.

'You're right,' Pike said. 'You ain't ever coming back.'

Ronald gulped, fear clawing at his belly. 'I'm doing what Nixon asked. I'm not strutting around town like Sherman or drinking the saloon dry like Chester. If you want to threaten anyone, threaten them.'

Hyde chuckled. 'We'll deal with them, but we're just making sure you keep your promise that you ain't *ever* coming back.'

Hyde's words were uttered with such finality that Ronald was tempted to swing his horse around and gallop away, even if it took him back to White Ridge, but instead he forced himself to move on.

He kept his gaze set straight ahead, not looking at either of Nixon's hired guns as he passed. Then he kept going at a steady pace, a silent prayer on his lips that they'd let him leave with their threats being just a final warning. He'd covered fifty yards and was beginning to breathe more easily when he heard hoofbeats closing from behind.

He tried to ride on as if nothing untoward was happening, but panic plucked at his already taut nerves and he spurred his horse. It had covered only a few galloped strides when hot fire punched him in the back, pushing him forward from his mount.

He fell. Then a second shot tore into his chest and he never stopped falling.

Presently the two hired guns drew up to look down at the body.

'Guess he ain't ever coming back,' Pike said.

'That ain't a problem,' Hyde said. 'He wouldn't have voted for Nixon.'

They'd come for him, as Jim McGuire had known they would.

It'd been only a few hours since his first attempt at speech-making and after getting a taste for publicly stating his opinion, three more speeches had soon followed, each growing in confidence and each getting more critical of Nixon. The final one earlier this evening in the saloon even gathered considerable support for his opinions on the way Nixon dealt with justice in White Ridge. So Jim had expected that this meeting would come shortly afterwards, but he still stayed sitting at the table facing the door.

The Peacemaker he hadn't fired in anger for the

last nine months lay before him on the table. He had finished cleaning and oiling the weapon, a ritual he performed every night despite the resolutions he'd made.

His only acknowledgement of the man he had once been was to swing the barrel round to face the door, then to place his right hand on the table beside the gun. He waited, listening to the sounds of men dismounting outside, then pacing to the door.

A grunted conversation took place outside, the words spoken too quietly for him to hear. Then the door slowly swung open to reveal Mayor Jake Nixon. Flanking him as always were Pike and Hyde.

As they entered, all three men's gazes took in the gun on the table before Nixon looked up to transfix Jim with his cold gaze.

'You're deriding me in public,' Nixon said, coming straight to the point, then he glanced at each of his hired guns. 'Something nobody else has dared to do.'

Jim nodded, deciding this comment meant that Nixon must be confident he could frighten off the other three candidates. In fact, he might have done that already.

'But now that someone has,' he said, 'you'll lose.'

Mayor Nixon took a short step towards him, his feigned jovial mood snapping away in an instant.

'As you like plain speaking, Jim McGuire, I'll give it to you plain. You will no longer speak out against me.'

Jim leaned forward and edged his hand towards his gun, the movement being noticed by the hired guns who both twitched their hands a mite closer to their holsters.

'Or?'

'Or you'll follow Ronald Malone out of town.'

Jim looked down at the gun on the table, then smiled.

'I ain't leaving,' he said, keeping his tone pleasant. 'So do you want to risk finding out whether I can pick up this gun and kill you before either of your gun-toting aides can take me out?'

Nixon considered Jim's confident demeanour.

'I don't.' Nixon widened his eyes. 'Because I know you can do it.'

'Then why are you threatening me?'

'For the same reason.' Nixon took a long pace up to the table, then slowly moved his hands to grip the edge and leaned forward to look Jim in the eye. 'And if you stop speaking out against me, the people in this room will be the only people who'll ever know you could do it.'

The first tremor of concern rippled through Jim's guts but he still asked the question that Nixon wanted him to ask, and for which he was relishing the answer he would receive.

'What do you mean?' he said.

'It means that six months ago a man who called himself Jim McGuire returned to his home town of White Ridge. Nobody remembered him, but despite the behaviour of the young man in his charge, he became a stalwart member of my town. But then one day he made the mistake of thinking he was so stalwart that people would listen to him.'

Jim smiled as Nixon eventually turned to the reason why he'd spoken out in the first place.

'I only want justice for Billy Jameson. Tell Sheriff Price to find the real murderer. Then I'll stop speaking out against you.'

'Billy won't escape the gallows and the reason why has nothing to do with Price or me. It's you. Because what will everyone think when they discover that the man supporting Billy is every bit as murderous as Billy is?' Nixon threw back his head and laughed, the sound forced and sneering. 'Jim McGuire, formerly known as Luther Mallory, a man who, some say, was one of the finest manhunters who ever lived.'

'*The* finest,' Jim said.

Nixon acknowledged Jim's admission of his past with a cold smile, then stood up straight.

'Except something happened to make you hang up your gun. You changed your name, came here with young Billy Jameson, then—'

'Then shot you to hell to stop you talking.'

Nixon shook his head. 'You don't think I'd come here to face you without insurance, do you? The evidence of your former life is hidden away in my lawyer's office. If I don't return, even that idiot Sheriff Price will be alert enough to understand its significance.'

Nixon raised his eyebrows, requesting a response, but Jim firmed his jaw and let the moment drag out before he provided the only answer he could.

'I won't speak out against you no more.' Jim moved

his hand away from his gun, making the hired guns relax.

Nixon pointed a firm finger at him. 'See that you keep that promise or I'll get the word out that you're here. Your enemies are wondering where you went to ground, so your new life will end with you being shot to pieces by whoever will pay the most to know where you are.'

With that threat, Mayor Nixon backed away to the door. Pike and Hyde remained to posture, feigning an arrogant, unconcerned air that Jim knew they didn't feel before they slipped outside, leaving him alone.

When he'd heard them ride away, Jim placed a hand on the gun, then spun it. He watched it turn, then slow to a halt. It stopped with the barrel pointing at the door and at the recently departed Nixon, making Jim smile.

'Except,' he said to himself, 'speaking out ain't the only way to beat you.'

'Get up, you good-for-nothing varmints!' Sheriff Price shouted. 'You've got some good news you don't deserve.'

Barney Dale swung his legs down from his cot and stretched while he watched the lawman make his way down the row of cells in the jailhouse, rattling the bars to ensure he had the prisoners' attention.

'Good news?' the prisoner in the last cell, Billy Jameson, said. 'I could do with some of that.'

Price stopped in front of his cell and frowned.

'I'm afraid the good news is for everyone else, Billy.'

He turned his back on Billy and faced the other prisoners. 'This morning you're getting a pardon.'

Price waited with his hands raised and his expression set in a fixed grin, awaiting the enthusiastic response, but he didn't get it.

'That ain't funny,' Barney said.

'It ain't, because it's true. Mayor Nixon's ordered me to clear out the jailhouse.' He gestured at Billy. 'Aside from this one.'

Two of the seven prisoners whooped with delight, but the rest were as sceptical as Barney was.

'Why?' Barney asked, speaking for them all.

'Because while you've been festering away in there, you won't have noticed that there's an election coming up.' Price moved to unlock Barney's cell. 'I guess the mayor must be getting worried if he needs seven extra voters.'

'He's sure got my vote,' one prisoner declared.

'But not mine,' Barney said. 'I don't live here.'

Price stopped with the key half-turned, making Barney gulp when he realized his mistake.

'I'd forgotten that,' Price said. 'Perhaps Nixon had too.'

'I'm just too damn honest,' Barney grumbled. 'That's my trouble.'

'You're just too damn talkative. That's your trouble.' Price turned the key and swung open the cell. 'But I'm looking forward to a peaceful week without you lot littering up my jailhouse, so if you don't tell him you were passing through, I won't remind him.'

Barney breathed a sigh of relief, although he still

25

hurried out of the cell before Price changed his mind. When the other prisoners had emerged, he filed in at the back and gave the remaining prisoner a supportive thumbs-up signal, but the morose Billy ignored him.

Five minutes later the newly freed prisoners were outside and drawing their first taste of freedom into their lungs. Walter Fenton was waiting for them and, as expected, their first duty was to pay the price of that freedom.

One by one Barney's fellow ex-prisoners lost no time in assuring Walter that they would do what was required by staying out of trouble and voting the right way at the end of the week. Barney kept back to prepare his own response, so when Walter moved on to him he put on his most trustworthy expression.

'I've learned my lesson and I'll be no trouble, no trouble at all,' he said, holding his hat before him and running it through his fingers. 'And I'll vote for Nixon come next week, no trouble, no—'

'But there is trouble,' Walter said. 'You don't live here.'

'That don't matter to me. I like Nixon so much I'll still vote for him.'

'Pleased to hear it, but only registered citizens of White Ridge can vote.' Walter paused, making Barney worry that he wouldn't be getting the freedom that was now tantalizingly close. 'But not to worry. On election day not everyone who wants to vote for Nixon will have the time to cast their vote, will they?'

'They won't,' Barney said, judging that no other

answer was required.

'So come next week, seek me out and I'll tell you the name of someone who can't get to cast his vote. Then you can help him out.' Walter reached down to the carpetbag at his feet and briefly opened it, letting Barney see that inside there were numerous large wads of bills. 'And for your trouble, you'll get a dollar.'

'A dollar for five minutes' work!' Barney leaned forward. 'How many times can I vote?'

CHAPTER 4

'I'm sorry,' Jim McGuire said, facing Billy Jameson through the cell bars in the otherwise prisoner-free jailhouse. 'I'm not opposing Nixon no more.'

Billy drew his legs up to his chin on his cot.

'Is that because he's released the other prisoners and proved you were wrong about him being too harsh?'

Jim smiled. Despite his surly and lazy manners, Billy was perceptive. The reason why Nixon had released the prisoners was the main talking point in town. Nobody was sure about his reasoning, but Billy had worked it out on his own.

'That's why he did it, for sure, but it won't work when I stop campaigning for the townsfolk not to vote for Nixon, but to support Sherman Donner.'

Jim knew he was taking a risk with his response to Mayor Nixon's threat, but it was a risk he had to take if he was to get Billy freed.

'But Sherman also reckons I'm. . . .' Billy trailed off when he saw that Jim was smiling, then lowered his legs to the floor and returned a smile for the first time. 'You've done a deal?'

Jim nodded. 'It's the way things are done in White Ridge. The price of my support for Sherman, both verbal and financial, is that when he becomes mayor he'll review Price's evidence. You'll be free within the hour.'

Billy considered that information, his expression returning to its previous sombre state.

'But Mayor Nixon has this election sewn up. Even with you supporting him how can Sherman win?'

Jim forced himself to continue smiling, not wanting Billy to spend what would be his last week in jail, one way or the other, worrying about something he couldn't change.

'Don't worry, Billy. I have plenty of ideas to help Sherman. So keep that chin up for another week and then you'll be one step closer to freedom.'

'Or one step closer to the gallows,' Billy murmured, looking down at the cell floor.

Then he looked up to give Jim a brief smile and nod that made Jim wish he'd been more realistic with his promises.

'I've got another seven votes,' Barney Dale proclaimed, rocking from foot to foot outside the mayor's office in his eagerness to get paid for today's work.

'That makes twenty-one,' Walter Fenton said, smiling encouragingly. 'You sure have become an asset to Nixon's campaign.'

'I'm trying to be. And for a dollar a name, I'll find you another fifty come next week.'

'And, of course, you'll tell me the names of anyone who is sure to vote for Sherman Donner.' Walter winked. 'Perhaps they might be *persuaded* to change their minds.'

Barney had already guessed that that might be Walter's attitude towards securing votes. But he'd already put that worry from his mind and instead was concentrating his thoughts on that carpetbag full of money.

'Perhaps they might,' he said. He turned to go, but Walter slapped a hand on his shoulder halting him, then beckoned for him to follow him into the mayor's office.

'Come,' Walter said. 'It's time you met the man for whom you're campaigning so diligently.'

Barney always avoided meeting important people, but he accepted that sometimes the price of easy money was to let his face become recognized.

The inside of the office was as grand as he'd expected. Over the wide and ornate desk behind which Nixon sat there was a large window that provided an elevated view down White Ridge's main thoroughfare. Nixon looked up and on seeing his visitor was Walter he registered his disappointment with a sneer.

'Get out,' he muttered. 'I'm expecting Sherman.'

To date Barney had been honest and noted only the names of people who had said they intended to vote for Nixon. But for a dollar a name, each time he'd received a different answer he'd been tempted to record the name nevertheless.

One look at the cold-eyed mayor, then another at the other man in the room, the stocky Deputy Carter, who was exuding quiet menace from beside the slightly open door to the adjoining office, convinced him that he should resist temptation.

'I won't be long,' Walter said with a pronounced gulp. 'This is Barney Dale, one of your new employees. He's gathered more votes today than I've secured in the last week.'

Nixon narrowed his eyes as he appraised Barney.

'Nobody gathers a vote until it's cast. I hope you are paying him on that basis.'

Walter nodded, confirming Barney's worst fear that payment wouldn't be forthcoming today.

'Although,' Barney said, stepping forward, 'I would welcome a small advance – for my hard work so far.'

'Many people would welcome that.' Nixon flashed a smile that didn't change the coldness in his eyes. 'But rest assured that I never forget a *friend*.'

Nixon's emphasis, backed up by his casual glance at Deputy Carter, suggested the opposite was also true, so Barney decided this was a good time to be quiet and let Walter do all the talking.

'And Barney,' Walter said, simpering, 'might be useful in many ways. He's one of the men you released from jail this morning and he's proved himself to be a model citizen.'

'I am pleased. What was his crime?'

'He's a thief.'

'Was,' Barney added, and put on what he hoped was an honest smile.

Nixon stared hard at him, so Barney filled in the ensuing silence by murmuring his thanks, but the arrival of Sherman Donner saved him from further scrutiny.

'I've come as you asked,' Sherman said, ignoring Barney and Walter as he paced up to the desk. 'What do you want?'

Nixon raised a hand, signifying he would answer that question shortly, then turned to Deputy Carter.

'See that we're not disturbed,' he said. He didn't deign to look at Barney or Walter again.

Out in the corridor Barney strained his hearing to listen to the conversation that started up, hoping he might learn something to his advantage, but he couldn't make out what they were saying.

The three men set off for the stairs at the end of the corridor, but halfway down the corridor Walter came to a sudden halt. He patted his pockets. Then, with a mumbled comment to Carter, he retraced his steps.

The deputy cast a bemused look at him, but when Walter slipped into the office beside the mayor's office, he grunted to himself then followed. Like Nixon, Carter ignored Barney and when he'd headed into the office, Barney found himself alone in the corridor.

Still hoping he might overhear something of interest he followed them back down the corridor. Unfortunately, they had left the office door open, ensuring he couldn't get close enough to the door to the mayor's office to listen without risking being seen.

He put on a wide smile in case he was seen, his excuse for his actions already on his lips. Then he glanced inside, but what he saw in there made all thoughts of listening in on Nixon's private conversation flee from his mind.

Deputy Carter had placed the carpetbag he'd seen yesterday on a desk and Walter was rummaging inside. From the way the sides of the bag bulged, Barney reckoned the bag was just as full of wads of bills as it had been during his brief glimpse of its contents yesterday.

He darted back a pace from the door, his fingers itching with anticipation and his mind working quickly. A dollar a name for a week was profitable work, but he hadn't been given a cent yet and the possibility of getting his hands on that bag had become a more tempting proposition.

A quick survey of the corridor confirmed there were no other doors, only the flight of stairs at the end. There were no hiding-places here, except for one. . . .

Barney crossed his fingers and calmly walked past the open doorway without looking in. He carried on to stand beside Nixon's door. When the two men emerged they only had to look his way to see him, but Barney put his hopes in them not doing that.

Presently nearing footsteps sounded within the room and Walter and Carter emerged. Walter had lowered his head while fingering through the wad of bills he'd claimed from the bag and the deputy walked looking straight ahead with stiff-backed authority.

33

Barney gulped involuntarily, the sound feeling as if it were loud enough to alert them, but they carried on down the corridor to the stairs. Their pace was slow, making Barney's heart hammer, but they disappeared from view without looking back.

Still, Barney continued to be cautious and tiptoed to the top of the stairs. When he looked down them he saw a truncated view of Walter's form passing through the door to head outside. Carter stayed in the corridor, guarding the door against unwanted visitors. This meant Barney would have to find a way past him after he'd stolen the carpetbag, but that was a problem to be solved later.

Barney hurried back to the office. A quick search of the desk revealed that the large bottom drawer was locked, but a blunt letter-opener that he found on the desk made quick work of the lock. Then he prised open the drawer to reveal the bulging bag.

A low whistle escaped his lips when he opened the bag, which made him remember that the door to the adjoining mayor's office was open. He looked up and was thankful to find that through the gap he couldn't see anyone and could hear only Nixon and Sherman talking in low tones.

He rummaged through the wads of bills, his practised eye calculating that there were several thousand dollars inside, which made the risk he was taking well worth it. He removed the bag, quietly closed the drawer, then scurried to the door to the corridor, but just as he was about to leave, Nixon's raised voice cut through the silence.

'What are you doing?'

Barney froze, devising then rejecting several explanations to excuse his actions, but then he realized that the voice had come from some distance away. With hope in his heart he turned and was relieved to find he was alone in the office. Nixon had been speaking to Sherman.

'I'm doing what I have to do to win this election,' Sherman replied, his voice also raised, 'for the good of all the people of White Ridge.'

Nixon snorted. 'That's what Ronald Malone said, but he ain't around no more.'

Barney was minded to leave while Nixon was otherwise engaged. But as he didn't have a plan to escape from the building and he was still curious as to what Nixon and Sherman were discussing, he headed to the door.

He stood beside it and peered through the thin crack between the door and the jamb, moving from side to side until he was able to see the two men. Nixon was still sitting behind his desk and Sherman was standing before the desk, gesticulating angrily.

'I came here to reach an understanding, not to hear more threats.' Sherman slammed a fist on the desk. 'You've said nothing that'll persuade me not to stand against you.'

Nixon leaned over the desk. 'Then try this – you won't win. You're risking your life unnecessarily.'

Sherman uttered a brief laugh. 'You're wrong. Despite the intimidation and the bribes, or maybe because of them, the tide is turning against you.

Before, three candidates split your opposing vote. Now that you've frightened off Ronald Malone and Chester Heart, that opposition is unifying behind one man – me.'

'Nobody but you will speak out against me again.'

'I know you persuaded Jim McGuire to be quiet.' Sherman leaned forward. 'Luckily for me.'

The smile that had been emerging on Nixon's face at the mention of McGuire's name died.

'What do you mean?'

'I mean you made a big mistake when you threatened a man like Jim McGuire. Before he was being only mildly effective, saying you shouldn't be mayor, but now I have his personal support and his financial backing.'

Nixon waved his arms, his face reddening.

'Don't trust the word of that . . . that. . . .'

'That former gunslinger, were you going to say?' Sherman smiled. 'He's told me about his past and it doesn't concern me. I've agreed that when I become mayor I'll free Billy Jameson. Then I'll appoint a proper lawman who will find out what really happened to Orson Brown.'

Sherman turned away, leaving Nixon glaring at his back, his face darkening by the moment. Then with a great roar Nixon leapt to his feet, knocking over his chair, and launched himself over the desk. His hands came up, clawlike, to wrap themselves around Sherman's neck from behind, his momentum making both men crash to the floor.

His attack was so sudden it made Barney dart back

from his observation point. He glanced at the open door to the corridor, thinking that he'd now seen and heard enough as, from within the main office, the sounds of struggling came to him. Voices were being raised. Furniture toppled. A pained scream tore out, quickly cut off.

This last noise made Barney put his eye to the gap again, to see that Mayor Nixon had pinned Sherman Donner to the floor. He was sitting on his chest with his hands wrapped around his throat while forcing down on his neck so strongly that his own eyes were popping and the cords stood out on his neck. Sherman battered Nixon's arms weakly but he couldn't force them away.

Footsteps pounded up the stairs, then down the corridor as the scream alerted Carter. The deputy would be sure to see Barney as he passed the door, so Barney had no choice but to hurl himself to the floor and roll into hiding behind the desk, where he tucked himself up underneath.

The door to the mayor's office slammed open.

'What the—?' Carter shouted.

'Damn varmint wouldn't listen to sense,' Nixon said, his voice emerging in short gasping bursts.

'Is he dead?'

Shuffling sounded. 'Sure is.'

'This ain't good.'

Nixon coughed then uttered a long sigh.

'Your talent for understatement usually amuses me, but not today. To lose two candidates was unfortunate, but to lose a third. . . .'

37

'What do you want me to do?'

'Get me out of here without anyone seeing me, then find an excuse for all this.'

Under the desk in the other office, Barney punched the air with delight, figuring he could escape in the confusion, but then he let his hand open when Carter replied:

'I'll fetch the bag. I reckon the money will provide all the excuses you'll need.'

CHAPTER 5

'And so,' Mayor Nixon announced to the crowd gathered outside the mayor's office, 'it gives me no pleasure to declare that this week's elections will not be the triumph for democracy we had hoped to enjoy.'

On the podium Nixon lowered his head, the action causing a ripple through the crowd as everyone followed his lead. At the back of the crowd Jim McGuire kept his head raised, looking for anyone who might not look as disturbed by the afternoon's events as everyone else was.

Jim had yet to hear the full story of what had happened, but he'd gathered that Walter Fenton had returned to the mayor's office to find Sherman Donner's dead body lying inside. There was also a problem concerning missing money, which might explain the reason for his murder. Not that Jim had any faith that the inept Sheriff Price would be able to work it out.

So he considered Nixon, then the bumbling lawman, then the other men on the podium, most being Nixon's hired guns.

But no matter how much he wanted to believe that the responsibility for Sherman's death lay with these men, he couldn't believe Nixon would be so brazen as to have him killed in his own office. Nixon didn't work in such an open way.

On the podium Nixon raised his head and the first person he looked at was Jim. For several seconds they exchanged eye contact, then Nixon coughed, drawing everyone's attention back to him.

'Sundown approaches,' he said, looking at the large orange ball of the sun, bleeding its last rays down the length of the road. 'Unless anyone declares his intention to stand within the next few minutes, I will regrettably accept that my appointment is to be uncontested. But the first act of my new term will be to task Sheriff Price with finding my opponent's killer. In fact, such is my determination, I will post a two-thousand-dollar reward from my own pocket.'

This declaration gathered a ripple of approval, after which Nixon folded his arms and looked at the setting sun, waiting to see if anyone would stand against him.

Nobody moved. But then again it wasn't likely that anyone would. The only other potential candidates were Ronald Malone, who had left town in a hurry yesterday, and Chester Heart, who was in the saloon, where he'd been in residence ever since Nixon and his hired guns had talked to him.

As the sun slowly set Jim's neck warmed and his heart beat faster with the recollection that he had enjoyed speaking publicly yesterday. In his former life

40

his work had been solitary and often secret, but if he was to make his new life in White Ridge work, for both himself and Billy, remaining in the background might not be possible. So although he didn't know whether Nixon had been behind his rival's murder, he was sure of one thing: he couldn't allow this to go on.

He raised a hand. He was at the back of the crowd and so his movement caught the attention only of the men on the podium. He moved to wend his way to the front, but before he'd taken a single step a solid object was thrust into the small of his back.

He hadn't realized that someone had been standing behind him. He had just started to turn when Mitch Hyde's gruff voice muttered in his ear.

'Stay,' he said. 'Nixon's got plans for you and they don't involve you standing against him.'

Jim stood straight. 'Killing me after Sherman's demise won't look good for Nixon.'

'You're wrong. It won't look good for you when we tell everyone you killed Sherman.' Hyde dug in his gun for added emphasis. 'With your past, who'll not believe us?'

Jim noted that this intervention had perhaps helped to confirm what he suspected had happened to Sherman, but he had to accept that he was the only one who knew this, for now. So he gave a rueful nod and raised his hands slightly, confirming he wouldn't try to reach the podium.

Hyde kept the gun pressed against his back, in case he should be tempted to make a sudden declaration, as the red sheen playing over the tops of the buildings faded. Slowly the last sliver of the sun closed to noth-ing on the horizon.

Jim had to admit this was one battle he couldn't win, so he started to turn his mind to how he would prove Nixon was behind Sherman's killing.

For his part, Nixon watched him, his interest making several people turn to look at Jim. Nixon looked away, then flinched. He stared intently over the heads of the crowd, his reaction making others turn.

Jim looked over his shoulder to see that a man was striding purposefully towards the podium from the stables. He was rangy, black-clad but trail-dirty, his hat pulled down low, letting Jim see only his firm and clean-shaven jaw. He parted the people before him like a stick drawn through water until he stood before Nixon.

'I,' he said with a firm and authoritative voice and a glance at the last spark of the fading sun, 'will stand against you.'

'I've never seen you before,' Nixon said. 'Only the townsfolk of White Ridge can stand for mayor.'

'I know.' The man stood with his feet planted wide apart as around him people murmured to each other, everyone broadly saying the same thing: that they'd never seen this man before.

'Then if you claim to be from around these parts, who are you?'

The man turned on the spot to look around the gathered people, his gaze seeming to rest on Jim for longer than was necessary, before he turned back to

Nixon. He reached into his pocket and withdrew an envelope, which he held up to Nixon.

'Read this,' he said.

Nixon reached down. He held the envelope at arm's length, then flicked it open and withdrew a single sheet of paper. With an embarrassed cough, he looped spectacles around his ears and began reading.

His right eye twitched and he darted his head up to look at Jim, then coughed again and replaced the paper before handing the envelope back to the man.

'It would appear that everything is in order and we are to have a contested election, after all.' He coughed. 'So, what name would you like to appear on the ballot papers?'

'Isaiah Jones,' the man said. 'And may the best man win.'

Then he gave a curt bow and turned on his heel. Without acknowledging anyone he walked through the crowd and headed back down the road to the stables.

Everyone watched him leave while murmuring about this unexpected occurrence. Jim also kept his eye on him but before Isaiah reached the stables Hyde nudged him forward.

'Move,' he grunted in his ear.

Five minutes later Jim stood in the mayor's office, noting the signs of the disturbance that had taken place in here a few hours earlier: the upturned furniture, a smashed chair, papers littering the floor. But through the open door to the adjoining office he could see that the mess in the main office was as nothing to what had happened in there.

The room had been ransacked with folders strewn everywhere, padded chairs had been sliced open, and a desk had been smashed so completely it might have been accomplished with an axe. His silent guard provided no answers as to what had happened here as they waited for Nixon, who arrived fifteen minutes later in surprisingly good spirits. Even the accompanying Pike was grinning.

'Are you confident of beating Isaiah?' Jim asked, letting sarcasm creep into his voice.

'Of course,' Nixon said. 'A man nobody knows standing against me is ideal. It provides competition without there being any real competition.'

'Then perhaps his arrival wasn't so unexpected, after all.'

Nixon's beaming smile suggested Jim had guessed wrong.

'You have a politician's mind, but no, I didn't hire him. Not that that should concern you as your involvement in this election has ended, but your involvement in something altogether more important is about to start. I want you to find Sherman's killer.'

Jim had expected to be threatened again, so this comment surprised him. He paced over to the window to look down on the road below. While he composed himself, he casually searched the road for any sign of the mysterious Isaiah.

'I can do that without leaving this office.'

Nixon snorted, then came over to stand beside Jim.

'I'll let that insult pass.'

44

Jim shrugged, not committing himself to believing anything yet.

'Orson Brown's death aside, my manhunting days are over. I'll leave it to Sheriff Price.' Jim turned and looked Nixon up and down. 'He can find the man responsible.'

'I see our recent disagreement hasn't dulled your sense of humour. Sheriff Price is useful for many things, none of which has anything to do with keeping law and order.' He gestured towards his hired guns. 'Pike and Hyde deal with the petty crime in White Ridge, but for the more specialist work, I hand-pick the right man for the job. You are that man.'

'I may be, but why do you really want to find the killer of a man you hated so much some even think you killed him yourself?'

'I don't care who killed him. I'd gladly offer a two-thousand-dollar reward, not to the man who tracks down his killer, but to the killer himself. But I'm not free to speak my mind. As people already suspect I had something to do with it, I can't let that gossip build. Find the killer and it'll silence any dissent.'

'After hearing that, you expect me to help you?'

'I do, because you did like Sherman and you can find his killer for the right reason.' Nixon looked at Jim until he shook his head, then resumed speaking. 'And if you won't do it for the right reason, do it to silence me.'

'You used that threat yesterday and it loses more of its power every time.'

'I know. So this is the last time. Find him and I'll give

you something you'll appreciate more than money. I'll give you the wanted posters, the newspaper articles, the statements, every detail that ties you to the man you once were. I'll let you become the man you want to be.'

Jim shrugged. 'My life is not as important as Billy Jameson's freedom.'

Nixon pouted, his minimal reaction suggesting he'd already considered that Jim would ask for this.

'Why is a former gunslinger so obsessed with this young man's life?'

Jim's heart beat faster as Nixon asked the question he'd never answered honestly, and which he even avoided thinking about himself.

'He's the son of an old friend,' he said, providing the excuse he always uttered when pressed.

'And Orson Brown was my friend. His paper supported me through my first eight years of service. Someone must pay for his death.'

'As he was your friend, you must want the right man to pay.'

'I believe Billy is that man.' Nixon rocked his jaw from side to side. 'So I won't free him, but if you find Sherman's killer before I'm re-elected, I'll delay his trial for a month. Find anything in that month to prove someone else did it and I'll free him. Otherwise he can take his chances in a court of law.'

Jim narrowed his eyes as Nixon offered tempting terms too readily, but he figured that the only way he could find out whether the duplicitous mayor would honour his agreement was by completing his side of the bargain.

'I was a manhunter, not a lawman. I always had a name.'

Nixon uttered a snorting laugh now that he knew he had him.

'You have a name – Barney Dale. This morning he was a prisoner, but after I opened the jailhouse doors he wormed his way into my confidence, then ransacked the office and stole several thousand dollars.'

'The reward offer, I presume?'

'It is,' Nixon said proudly. 'So will you accept my assignment?'

Jim breathed in deeply through his nostrils and looked down into the road as if he were pondering.

'I'll bring Barney Dale in.'

'Dead or alive, it matters none to me.'

'Then it'll be alive. In my former life I wouldn't have cared, but this time I'll do it the proper way and ensure Sherman gets justice in court.'

'That is your concern, but remember that I'm not a man who accepts failure.' Nixon turned away to beckon his hired guns. 'So to ensure you have all the help I can offer, my trusted workers Pike and Hyde will accompany you.'

The hired guns maintained their bored expressions as they came over, suggesting this assignment wasn't news to them.

'I don't need them,' Jim said. 'I work alone.'

'Before, you worked alone.' Nixon turned back and smiled. 'Now, you work for me.'

47

CHAPTER 6

'Can I ask a question?' Sheriff Price said, while he sidled across the ransacked mayor's office to join Pike and Hyde.

Nixon looked away from his consideration of the hired guns and gave the sneer he always plastered over his face when he was dealing with Price.

'In a moment.' Nixon pointed at the door to the other office. 'Stand over there while I finish my business.'

'Thank you,' Price murmured. Then, like an errant child, he meekly shuffled over to stand beside the door. To avoid the mocking grins all three men were casting at him, he concentrated on examining the mess next door.

'Any clues as to where Barney Dale went?' Nixon asked Pike.

'Jim McGuire asked around,' Pike said. 'He found someone who saw him hightailing it out of town going west. Jim reckons he'll have gone to Milton Creek.'

'And you?'

'Got no reason to disagree,' Pike grumbled. 'He is

the finest manhunter who ever lived, after all.'

Pike's sneering tone made Nixon chuckle.

'Don't be aggrieved that I hired Jim. I had to take this opportunity to stop him being a thorn in my side during my election campaign. So keep your temper and don't let him out of your sight until he finds Barney.'

'And then?'

Nixon cast a quick glance at Price then lowered his voice and spoke with a deliberate slow pace.

'I will go on record as saying I will be concerned if anything should happen to either Barney or Jim and they fail to return to White Ridge.'

'Understood,' Pike said. Then he and Hyde turned on their heels and left the office.

Nixon turned to look at Sheriff Price and waited for him to state his business.

Price tried not to think too much about the conversation Nixon had had with Pike and Hyde. Prying too much always made Nixon angry. He pointed into the adjoining office while walking to the desk.

'I still don't understand what happened in there,' he said.

'Why do you need to understand anything?' Nixon asked.

Nixon's stern gaze made Price gulp.

'Because. . . . Because I have to clarify the facts.'

'Then the instructions I gave to Pike and Hyde should have put your mind at rest. I am working out the details, as I did with Billy Jameson.'

'I know, but this time the circumstances aren't so

obvious and the suspect is still at large and. . . .' Price felt most of the confidence he'd plucked up to come here drift away and he lowered his head.

'And?'

'And. . . . And I reckon I ought to investigate this properly, if it's not too much trouble.'

Nixon curled his upper lip in a snarl, but a look at the heaps of paperwork on his desk made him wave at Price in a dismissive manner.

'Do what you have to do, Price, to ensure the legalities are dealt with. My men will bring Barney back within days. Make sure you get it over with by then.' Nixon pointed at the door. 'And keep out of my way.'

'I'll do that, Mayor, so if I could have a few more moments of your time now, you can tell me your story.'

'I've told you what I know already.'

Nixon glared at Price and his piercing gaze made Price's mouth go so dry it took him several moments before he could force himself to answer.

'You. . . . You did,' he stammered, 'but as I said, I don't understand it. Barney isn't a violent man.'

Nixon sneered. 'And you worked that out all by yourself, did you, while slopping out his cell?'

'I did. He's a habitual thief, but he doesn't carry a gun. His main weapon is his belief that he can talk himself in to any gainful situation and talk himself out of any trouble.'

Nixon dismissed the matter with a wave of the hand.

'The lack of a gun would explain why he strangled Sherman.'

'It could,' Price conceded, feeling the rest of his limited confidence drift away and making the rest of his comments emerge as a mumble. 'But it still doesn't feel right. Everyone has a different account of what happened.'

'I'm sure that once you have all the details,' Nixon said, lowering his voice, 'it'll become perfectly clear.'

Price caught the warning in his tone. He offered a tentative smile.

'I'm sure it will, so, if you don't mind, please, it would help me to start with what you did see, rather than what other people told you they saw.'

'Me?' Nixon narrowed his eyes. 'What are you saying, Price?'

'I'm not saying anything,' Price spluttered, suddenly seeing how Nixon could have viewed his innocent comment as a threat. 'It just might be . . . might be useful to know why Sherman came here.'

'I don't know. I wasn't here.'

'So where were you, if you don't mind me asking?'

For long moments Nixon considered Price over the top of his glasses, to ensure he understood that he had strayed too far with his insistent questioning.

'Price, you have supported me through two elections and when I have disposed of the small inconvenience of this Isaiah Jones we will enter a third term together. We have always got along because you don't ask questions.' Nixon pursed his lips, giving Price an opportunity to reply, but as Price's legs were shaking and he didn't think he could make himself speak, he continued: 'But as you wish to know where I was: I was talking with a good friend in private, ensuring I acquired his vote.'

'Who?' Price croaked.

'I will decide who that person should be and will ensure that by sundown you have a signed statement suitable to be read out in court. Where I actually was, is of no concern of any court.'

Price heard the more urgent warning in Nixon's lowered tone and so he chose his words carefully.

'Is it any concern of mine?'

'It is not. But as it appears that you feel you must know,' Nixon coughed, 'I was somewhere where many people know I frequent, but where many others don't; somewhere where it'd be embarrassing for the mayor to admit in court.'

'Ah,' Price said. 'The Pink Lady?'

'Exactly. So, is there anything more you wish to waste my time with, or can I get back to running my town?'

Price knew when he'd pushed Nixon's patience, and this time he'd strained it. He thanked him then left the office. But as he walked past the open door to the adjoining office he glanced in at the ransacked room.

'I still don't reckon,' he said to himself, 'that Barney Dale would make such a mess.'

'I want Barney Dale,' Pike said.

'Never heard of him,' the bartender said.

'He'd have come through Milton Creek in a hurry, perhaps with a . . .' Pike trailed off when the bartender shook his head.

'I don't know about no man in a hurry,' he said then picked up a glass and polished it vigorously.

Pike nodded. He turned as if he was about to leave the saloon, then swirled back and lunged over the bar to grab the bartender's chin. His move was so swift the bartender didn't have enough time to react other than to drop the glass.

The smashing of glass made the customers in the saloon room look up, but that didn't concern Pike as with his vicelike grip he dragged the bartender's head down to the bar to place his cheek to the wood.

'Now,' he muttered, glaring down at him, 'I'll ask you the question again and this time you'll answer me. I'm looking for Barney Dale.'

The bartender rocked an eye up to consider Pike then twitched as if trying to shake his head.

'I . . . I . . . I don't know nothing about this man.'

Pike's eyes flared and he closed his hand a mite, making the bartender bleat, but with customers scraping back their chairs, Jim moved in and slapped a hand on Pike's arm.

'Release him,' he said, then darted his gaze to the side.

Pike took in the aggrieved customers with barely a flicker of concern.

'I will, when I get me an answer.'

'Then we'll never leave. He doesn't know nothing about Barney.'

Pike and Jim locked gazes while around them muttering arose as the customers goaded each other on to be the first person to intervene. For several seconds Pike held on to the bartender's chin, then with a muttered oath he pushed him away. He faced the customers, his gaze cold.

'I'm looking for a Barney Dale,' he announced. 'So which one of you foul-smelling bunch of whiskey hounds knows where he's gone?'

Jim winced as Pike chose another method of questioning that was sure to fail, but he still looked along the line of men to see if any reacted with anything other than anger. But the customers just glanced at each other, to see who else was annoyed. And it appeared that most of them were.

As one the line of men paced towards the bar. On the second pace one man took a slightly longer movement so as to be the one who confronted Pike.

'We don't like—' he managed to say before Pike rocked forward and thundered a low punch into his guts that had him folding over. Then Pike slapped both hands on his back and threw him towards the bar. The man rolled over it to join the bartender.

'Anyone else?' Pike demanded, but the rest of the customers had already seen enough and as one they charged in.

Two men took on Pike but he slapped the first aside with contemptuous ease, then kicked the second man's legs from under him. Hyde took on the men nearest to him leaving Jim with no choice but to square up to the men at his end of the line.

He bided his time, letting them come to him and when the first man threw a huge haymaker of a punch he jerked aside to let his fist whistle through air. Then he swung round and delivered a short-arm jab to the man's kidneys that made him screech, then stagger away.

The second man was more cautious, waiting until he had help from a third man. Then they both charged at Jim with their heads down, but Jim had anticipated their actions.

He leapt to the side to meet the right-hand man full on, then grabbed this man around the shoulders and shoved him into the path of the left-hand man. Entangled, the men went down and with a satisfied grin to himself Jim stepped over them to face his next assailant. Then he flinched back in shock.

Everyone in the saloon had decided to join in the fray and a dozen more men were hurrying to the bar to take the strangers on. Worse, Pike and Hyde had already disappeared behind a mass of heaving bodies. Jim resigned himself to getting a beating while still being determined to give as good as he got. Then a gunshot blasted out.

For a moment everyone froze. Then the mass of men parted to reveal Pike standing with his gun thrust high, having fired into the ceiling.

'The next one will rip someone in two,' he roared, 'if I don't get me an answer.'

The line of surly glares Pike got in return suggested he wouldn't get what he wanted, but Jim could also see that several of the customers were armed and were twitching their hands towards their holsters.

He edged sideways to join Pike.

'They don't know nothing about Barney Dale,' he said from the corner of his mouth. 'We should leave them to their drinks.'

Pike snarled, his fiery gaze looking as if Jim would be the first one he turned his gun on, but to Jim's surprise Hyde nodded.

'Jim's right,' he said. 'We'll try somewhere else.'

Pike cast his surly glare along the line of customers, then sneered and spat on the floor.

'Yeah,' he said. 'The air in here is too foul for my stomach.'

With that last insult he turned on his heel and without looking again at the customers he walked to the door. Hyde and Jim shuffled after him, walking sideways to make sure the customers weren't willing to continue the fight, but with Pike having gone their annoyance left with him.

Jim and Hyde joined Pike out on the boardwalk, where they looked up and down Milton Creek's main thoroughfare, taking in the few buildings and the even fewer people going about their business.

'We were lucky to get out of there alive,' Jim said, still looking from the corner of his eye into the saloon to make sure nobody was following them out.

'They were the ones who got lucky,' Pike said. 'But perhaps you'd like to pick who I question next, seeing as how you know who has seen Barney and who hasn't.'

Despite the unnecessary fight in the saloon Jim understood Pike's irritation. If he'd guessed wrong in coming to Milton Creek, this could turn out to be a long manhunt. Normally that wouldn't have concerned him, but with the necessity of finding Barney within the week, he was as edgy as Pike felt, even if he didn't show it.

'Obliged for the offer,' Jim said, 'except this time I'll do the questioning. Then maybe we'll get to leave town without getting into another brawl.'

Pike looked Jim up and down, sneering.

'I thought you were the finest manhunter who ever lived.'

'I am, and I only became that by avoiding fights I didn't need.' With a waggle of a finger Jim beckoned for Pike and Hyde to follow him, then set off across the road. 'Watch, be quiet, and learn how it's done.'

Pike and Hyde grunted to each other about how they thought Jim was unlikely to succeed in getting answers where they'd failed, but they still followed him. Jim headed to Baxter's mercantile, which stood beside the stables and was the largest such establishment on the road.

Inside he wandered around the wares, keeping a pleasant smile on his face. Baxter emerged to appraise him, although he spent more time casting concerned looks at his surly-looking companions. Luckily, before his concern became too great, Jim found what he was looking for: a particularly fine-looking saddle.

He patted the leather, nodding approvingly, then looked at Pike and Hyde.

'I've found it,' he called out to them lightly.

Both men stared at him, silent and bemused, but this comment provided enough encouragement for

Baxter to come over.

'It's a mighty fine saddle,' he said.

'Sure is,' Jim said, keeping his tone conversational. 'My brother bought one just like it from you for his new horse. I thought I'd get myself one too.'

Baxter rubbed his hands. 'This one is nearly the same as the one I sold yesterday, but to be honest I reckon it's a whole lot finer.'

Jim stood back, nodding. 'I agree. I'm only buying a saddle, but I have to admit Barney sure did look mighty proud on his new steed. Do you know what I mean?'

'I agree. That black stallion deserved the best.'

'Barney always reckoned he deserved the best.' Jim glanced around the store, taking in the now intrigued Pike and Hyde. 'Did he get himself dandied up in here too?'

'Sure. I sold him a complete new set of clothes.'

'You did?' Jim punched the air then let a frown cross his features. He patted his jacket, then withdrew a handful of bills, which he glanced at before replacing them. 'Were they expensive?'

'Not too expensive,' Baxter said, grinning as the sight of the money removed the last shred of scepticism he had about the likelihood of a forthcoming sale. 'As I'm dealing with a man of your standing I'm sure we can discuss terms.'

'Then perhaps I can afford to buy what Barney had, after all. Which clothes did you sell him?'

'I'll show you,' Baxter said, hurrying behind the counter. He slipped into his back store, then edged his head out again and raised a hand. 'Don't go anywhere. I'll be back.'

'Take as long as you need,' Jim said pleasantly. Then, when Baxter had disappeared from view, he turned to Pike and Hyde and lowered his voice. 'We now know what Barney was wearing and what he was riding. After a few more friendly discussions, we'll know where he went too. And all without getting us into another fight. So, have you two learned anything yet?'

'I sure have learned something,' Pike grunted, then leaned to the side to spit on the floor. 'I'm now looking forward to getting this manhunt over with real quick.'

Beside him, Hyde added his own gob of spit before both men delivered low and snorted laughs.

CHAPTER 7

The rider was closing on the mound, but Jim McGuire had already noted the proud black stallion he was riding, and the clothes and new saddle they'd seen and heard about in Baxter's mercantile gleamed in the bright afternoon sunlight.

Best of all, the rider was paying no attention to the 200-foot-high rounded mound he was passing and so hadn't looked up to the top where Jim and his companions were watching him.

When he'd ridden to within 400 yards of the mound, Jim considered his next move. Despite the unwelcome presence of his two surly companions, he had enjoyed employing the old skills that had worked for him before. But the primary skill that'd kept him alive while working in a notoriously dangerous occupation was that he never took anything for granted. So he ordered Pike to get back from the edge of the mound and make his way down to ground level behind their approaching quarry.

'Why?' Pike said. 'He don't look like trouble.'

'He don't, but we're taking him alive and to be sure we get out of this alive too, we'll surround him before we move in.'

'Three of us running scared before a snivelling runt like Barney Dale,' Pike snorted. 'For the finest-ever manhunter, you sure are being cautious.'

'I became that by being cautious, but seeing as you asked so nicely, I'll explain what should have been obvious to you. Barney stole several thousand dollars from your boss. That's enough to buy protection. So we move in carefully in case that protection shows itself.'

This comment took the arrogant gleam out of Pike's eye. With a curt nod to Hyde he headed off down the mound. Then, without further comment, Hyde and Jim made their way down from the top of the mound using the cover of a gully.

They reached ground level a hundred yards ahead of the rider, remaining hidden throughout, and stopped beside a large sentinel boulder at the entrance to the gully. There, acting on Jim's whispered orders, Hyde glanced out, then darted back.

'He'll be here in a minute.' Hyde pointed, tracing the path Barney would take and showing that he'd pass them by some twenty yards from the boulder.

'Still alone?'

'Sure.' Hyde leaned back to peer up the side of the mound. 'I doubt Pike will find anyone. I reckon Barney is on his own.'

'Perhaps he is, perhaps he isn't. Neither of us will know for sure until it's too late.' Jim waited until Hyde muttered about him being too cautious before he continued: 'But sometimes, no matter how cautious you're being, you have to spring the trap, then see what happens.'

Hyde smiled. 'Glad we're thinking the same way for once.'

With that comment, Hyde raised a hand to his ear, listening to the approaching hoofbeats and counting down on his fingers. Then he swung out onto clear ground, not waiting for more instructions. Not that Jim would have provided any. He'd already gathered that his companions hadn't appreciated or learned anything from his subtle method of finding their quarry.

But this situation didn't call for subtlety and if Hyde wanted to risk himself by standing in the firing line of any hidden protection Barney might have arranged, Jim saw no reason to stop him.

'What you want?' a voice, presumably Barney's, called out.

Jim moved to higher ground so that he could see over the boulder. The rider had stopped fifty yards away from Hyde. To affect a successful capture this was further away than Jim would have liked, but they should be able to pin Barney down whether he had hidden help or not.

'Depends,' Hyde said. 'Are you Barney Dale?'

'Who wants to know?'

Jim observed that Hyde's hand was straying towards his holster, so he hurried down to ground level and paced out beyond the boulder.

'Mayor Nixon does,' he said. 'He's hired us to take you back to White Ridge to explain yourself.'

'Has he really?' Barney said. He looked at Jim then ran his gaze along the mound. 'Then I'd better come with you two.'

He rocked forward in the saddle, looking as if he was about to dismount, but then he hurled his hand to his gun while throwing himself from his horse. Two crisps shots rang out. Hyde's slug hurtled by Barney's tumbling form while Barney's kicked dirt a few feet behind Hyde.

Barney hit the ground on his side and rolled. Luckily, the gunfire spooked his horse. As Hyde darted from side to side trying to get a clear view of him, the horse reared, blocking his view and letting Barney scramble into cover. By the time the stallion had skittered out of the way he had gone to ground in a hollow in which he lay flat.

Hyde went to one knee and blasted lead at the hollow, probably more in frustration than to achieve anything, then darted a glance at Jim. With a few silent gestures Jim ordered him to stay where he was while he reached higher ground to get an angle on their target.

With a downward gesture of caution he also tried to convey that Hyde should remain calm. He still hoped to take Barney alive, but Hyde's steady glare suggested he wasn't prepared to listen.

He scurried back to the sentinel boulder and rolled himself on to the top to lie on his belly. This elevated position let him see Barney's form and Jim judged he could easily shoot him if it proved necessary.

He rested his gun hand on his forearm, noting that this was the first time for nine months that he had been prepared to shoot another man. But he shook the image of the previous man from his mind, an image that hadn't haunted him since he'd settled in White Ridge, and took careful aim. Then he spoke up.

'Barney!' he shouted. 'This is a hopeless situation. We have you covered. Come out now and you'll get to live for long enough to tell everyone your side of the story.'

Barney flinched, then looked up at the boulder. From fifty yards away Jim could judge from his jerky movements the thought processes that went through his mind; he wondered if he could turn a gun on him quickly, wondered if Jim's aim was sound.

'All right,' Barney said with a resigned sigh. 'This ain't my battle.'

Jim checked on Hyde, who was still kneeling poised with his gun trained on the hollow.

'Then throw out your gun, real slow.'

'I sure will. Just don't fire.'

Barney raised himself slightly to hurl the gun over-arm, but when his body was at its highest point a gunshot rang out from the mound.

Jim turned to see that Pike was making his way down to ground level, firing as he walked. His second slug tore into Barney's side and made him screech then roll to the side, coming to rest half-in, half-out of the hollow, his gun falling from his slack fingers.

Hyde took the opportunity to plant another bullet in him.

'Stop that!' Jim shouted, but both men fired again. This time the bullets merely thudded into Barney's supine form.

'Why did you do that?' Jim demanded.

'I thought he was going for another weapon,' Hyde said, pacing up to the hollow. He kicked Barney's unresponsive body in the chest, rolling him on to his front, then nodded approvingly and looked at Jim. 'You reckon we shouldn't have done that?'

Jim sighed, then jumped down from the boulder and made his way to the body. He confirmed that Barney had been killed.

'Anyone else out there?' he asked when Pike joined him.

'Nope,' Pike said. 'Caution weren't needed with this one.'

'And is that him?'

Pike considered Barney's body. 'I never saw him, but I reckon so.'

'Why?'

'Because he acted like an idiot who'd got himself some easy money. Then he left a trail so obvious even you could follow it.'

'He did, didn't he?' Jim mused. He gestured at the stallion. 'Get that horse back and see how much of the money is left to return to your boss.'

'Now that we've got Barney, you ain't ordering us around no more.' Pike licked his lips. 'You get the horse.'

Jim considered his arrogant companions, noting the sneaky glances they were casting at each other, as if Pike's demand contained an ulterior motive. Then he considered the body and the horse, while pondering on how easy it had been to find Barney. He smiled.

'I won't do that because I don't need to. I know what I'd find in the saddle-bags.' Jim raised his eyebrows. 'Nothing.'

'He can't have spent all that money already.'

'He can't.' Jim pointed at the body. 'Because, you see, the reason Barney didn't have any protection with him is because this man was his protection.'

'What you mean?'

'I mean he's a decoy. You two have just killed the wrong man.'

'We have him,' Pike grumbled, not for the first time since they'd set off from the mound. 'We don't need to go back to Milton Creek.'

Jim glanced at the body slung over the back of the stallion.

'Maybe we don't,' he said, 'but I'll leave you to explain yourself to Mayor Nixon if we've got the wrong man.'

As Jim's comment raised an appreciative chuckle from Hyde, he drew his horse to a halt and looked around. The railroad was to his left, a distant train making its slow way towards town. Milton Creek was a half-mile ahead.

'Why do you think our dead friend ain't Barney?' Hyde asked.

'Because there was no money in his saddlebags and because before you shot him to hell, he nearly got you.'

'Being able to spend quickly and shoot badly ain't much to base your belief on.'

'True, but from what I've learned about Barney it's enough for me. If you want to stop looking, that's your choice. I prefer to make sure.'

Jim noticed that Pike and Hyde glanced at each other before Hyde replied but, as on the previous occasions when they'd silently questioned each other, Jim didn't let on that he'd noticed.

'We stay together,' Hyde said. 'If you're not sure this body is Barney's, we carry on searching.'

Jim nodded, then moved his horse on to head into town. Hyde and Pike moved back to flank the body, presumably to guard it from casual sight, and presumably they were also prepared to frighten off anyone who did notice.

At their slow pace the train caught up with them as they entered town.

'So,' Pike asked as they passed the stables, 'where do we start looking again if you're so convinced we followed the wrong man?'

'Aside from avoiding the saloon I ain't sure yet, but the point is we didn't follow the wrong man. We followed the man we were supposed to follow, and that means Barney is cleverer than I thought.'

'Or you're more gullible than I thought.'

Jim conceded that point with a grunt, then drew his horse to a halt outside Baxter's mercantile, this being the mid-point in town.

'Anyone can complain,' he said. 'Offer suggestions or be quiet.'

So Pike provided his idea, after which he and Hyde went into the mercantile. While Jim waited for them to employ their usual methods, he looked up and down the main road, pondering.

Barney had appeared to be an easy subject to follow, being a petty thief who had killed while stealing. His actions had been predictable in that he wouldn't have been able to resist spending his loot.

But clearly he'd put more thought into his escape than Jim had given him credit for. Knowing a pursuit would ensue, he'd hired a decoy while he had made good his escape.

Jim had always enjoyed chasing the more ingenious quarries, but to catch them he needed to understand them well enough to second guess their next move. This time, with the deadline approaching fast he didn't have the luxury of time. He needed to follow a hunch.

As if in answer to his pondering, the train whistled as it drew to a halt in the station. He nodded to himself as Pike and Hyde emerged from the mercantile, flexing their fists.

'The dead man ain't the man Baxter sold the saddle to,' Pike reported. 'He doesn't know where the one he did sell it to went, but you were right. We got the wrong man and Barney is still on the run.'

Jim smiled. 'But perhaps he didn't go far. How often do the trains pass through Milton Creek?'

'Don't know,' Hyde said, 'once a week or so, I guess.'

'Then that's where he'll be.'

'How do you know that?'

'Any escape leaves a trail, so going nowhere often leaves the least clues. Or at least that's what I'd do if I were Barney.'

'You mean it's a guess?'

'I mean I'm using my experience.' Jim turned towards the station, but then turned back. 'But like I said, you don't have to stay with me. Follow your own hunches and use your own methods if you want to.'

'We don't,' Pike said. 'Our orders are to stay with you.'

Jim considered each man's blank and inscrutable expression. He wondered what else he could ask them to find out what their precise instructions were, but then shrugged and set off for the station.

'Just remember,' he said, 'this time we try to take him alive.'

'Of course,' Pike and Hyde said together.

Five minutes later they were installed on the train and fifteen minutes after it had left the station, Jim had proved beyond reasonable doubt that Barney Dale wasn't in the first two cars.

The description they had of him was a general one, so Jim had devised a plan to expose their target. He had removed the distinctive saddle from the stallion and taken it on board. Manoeuvring it down the aisle wasn't easy and the accompanying fuss made sure everyone noticed it.

So far nobody had reacted with anything other than irritation at having to move out of its way and none of them had shown a glimmer of recognition.

The lack of success made his surly companions cast glances at each other, but curiously he didn't detect that they were irritated by the possibility that they had wasted time in boarding the train.

Jim put that unresolved problem from his mind and headed into the third and last car. This time he kept the saddle held low so that the passengers wouldn't see it until he got close to them. There were a dozen people, each sitting alone, of whom half were either too old or women.

Jim made his slow way down the aisle and swung the saddle up on to the seat beside the first likely candidate. This man glanced at the saddle, then shuffled away from it. Jim judged that he hadn't been surprised to see it, so he moved on to the next one, who also reacted in the same way.

With a growing sense of unease Jim moved on through the remaining passengers, but each of them failed to show any interest in the saddle until he had just one person left to try.

He judged this man to be the same age as Barney Dale. He glanced at Hyde and Pike, who were already on alert with their hands close to their holsters, having decided this man was a strong candidate to be their target.

Jim kept his gaze on the passenger, making the man flinch, then look at him. At that moment Jim raised the saddle but the man gave it barely a glance before turning to resume looking out the window.

Jim blew out his cheeks in exasperation. Years of manhunting meant he prided himself on being able to read people and their expressions, but in his view this man and everyone else on the train had reacted without a hint of recognition.

He carried on through the door, then leaned on the rail looking down at the receding tracks and feeling foolish for having put his faith into what now seemed an overoptimistic plan. Hyde and Pike joined him.

'Your plan didn't work,' Hyde said in a matter-of-fact manner. 'Perhaps your subtle methods aren't so successful, after all. First, they led us to the wrong man. Now, they can't find the right man.'

Jim accepted this truth with a curt nod.

'I did put a lot of faith into that plan. But I'm sure there are other ways to work out which passenger is Barney.' He gestured back into the car. 'So we'll search the train again and this time more thoroughly. You two head on in there and go through the passengers one at a time.'

'And you?'

Jim hefted the saddle then shoved it into Hyde's chest, forcing him to grab hold of it.

'I'll cover your rear.'

With a glance at each other and a murmured grumble Hyde and Pike set off into the car. While Pike did the questioning, Hyde walked to the door at the opposite end of the car in case Pike alerted their quarry and he ran.

Jim watched through the window in the door, appraising Pike's unsubtle method, which involved barking a demand to know who each passenger was and not moving on until he had enough proof to satisfy him.

'You're on this train somewhere,' Jim said to himself. 'I'm sure of it.'

Slowly his gaze rose to consider the roof. A smile hovered on his lips.

He waited until Pike had moved on to his third passenger. Then he reached for the ladder leading to the roof and climbed up a few rungs until he was just below the rim. He bobbed up to look on to the roof.

Sure enough, his hunch proved to be right. On the roof a man was lying on his front facing away from him and looking down at the door at the opposite end of the car. His cocked head suggested he was listening.

Moving stealthily, Jim rolled himself on to the roof then stood in a stooped posture with his arms held wide for balance. Then he made his way towards the man. The rattling of the train masked the sounds of his progress, letting him get to within a few paces of the man before he moved. Then it was only to slip backwards because the door below was opening.

Jim hurried on, his gun coming to hand.

'Barney Dale?' he demanded, jabbing the gun into the back of the man's neck.

'What the. . . ?' The man flinched and twitched as if Jim had already shot him, forcing Jim to kneel on the small of his back to subdue him.

'Answer the question or you won't get to live for

long enough to return to White Ridge.'

'Would it help any if I said I'm not this . . . this Barney Yale?'

Jim snorted a laugh. 'That answer tells me everything I need to know.'

He raised his knee then tugged Barney's jacket to deposit him on his back. Barney considered Jim's firm glare then gave an apologetic shrug.

'I suppose I got as far as I could.' Barney patted his bulging pockets and well-padded jacket, presumably feeling the money he'd secreted about his person. 'Perhaps I should have invested in a gun, though.'

'It wouldn't have done you no good, bearing in mind the kind of men who're after you.'

'That's what I figured.' He considered Jim, recognition flashing in his eyes, although Jim couldn't remember seeing him before. 'I knew Nixon would send his hired guns after me, but I didn't think he could buy Jim McGuire.'

'He didn't. I'm ensuring justice is done for Sherman Donner so that. . . .' Jim trailed off, deciding he didn't need to explain himself.

From below he heard Hyde and Pike talking, hearing enough of their conversation to gather they'd heard him and Barney talking up on the roof. Quick orders barked out, followed by the door slamming shut.

Jim waited for one of them to appear on the roof but a minute passed without this happening, so he surmised they were being cautious for once.

'How will killing me get that justice?' Barney asked.

73

'I won't kill you if you don't give me no trouble. I'll ensure you get to stand before a court of law.'

Barney's eyes opened wide. 'A court of law! Because of the money that went missing?'

'For that, and for Sherman Donner's murder.'

'That had nothing to do with me. . . .' Barney slapped his forehead. 'But I should have known. All right. Get it over with and kill me or let those other two kill me. It'll stop me suffering.'

Pike's face appeared over the edge of the roof before jerking down. A few seconds later Hyde appeared. He also ducked down afterwards.

'Come up,' Jim shouted. 'I've got him.'

'Just do it quickly,' Barney said with a gulp, closing his eyes.

'Listen to me,' Jim snapped. 'I won't kill you, and if you didn't kill Sherman you've got nothing to fear from a court.'

Barney opened his eyes and transfixed Jim with what Jim took to be an honest gaze. When he spoke his tone was deep and serious.

'I have everything to fear because not only did I not kill Sherman Donner, I know who did kill him.'

Jim winced, the numerous anomalies that had occurred since Sherman's death falling into place instantly.

'Nixon?' he asked.

'Yup.'

'Can you prove it?'

'Nope. But I saw what happened. It's my word against his.'

'That's the word of the *respected* mayor against the word of a man who reckons he can talk his way out of any situation, is it? How do I know that's not what you're trying to do now?'

'You don't.' Barney looked at Hyde, who was rolling onto the roof closely followed by Pike. 'But I'll be dead in a few seconds. Then just before those two complete Nixon's orders and kill you, you'll have all the proof you need that Nixon doesn't want me brought to justice. He wants me silenced.'

Jim glanced at the hired guns. Both men were now standing on the roof, their right hands moving purposefully but still discreetly towards their holsters.

Jim had to admit that Barney's comments made sense. The hired guns hadn't tried to take the man he'd found alive. And they'd made no effort to find Barney on their own, preferring to stay with him and use his manhunting skills. . . .

Jim tightened his fists then nodded.

'I reckon you're right,' he muttered, then pushed Barney to the roof of the train while stepping forward and reaching for his gun.

Together the two approaching men drew their weapons, but Jim was faster, if not accurate. He fired twice, the first shot winging over Pike's shoulder and the second tearing splinters from the roof.

Both men returned fire but with the train rocking so much their shots also clattered feet wide of Jim and Barney. Despite everyone's inaccuracy in self-preservation, Pike and Hyde followed Barney's lead in dropping to the roof to present small profiles.

Jim took advantage of their caution by grabbing Barney's shoulder and dragging him away from them. Getting his meaning, Barney got to his feet and, hunched over, the two men backed away down the train with Barney slipping in behind Jim.

At the other end of the roof the two hired guns swung themselves round to lay head on to him with their guns thrust out straight ahead, using the solid roof to keep their hands steady. They took steady aim.

Jim twitched his gun a mite higher, meaning to return fire, but he was finding it hard to keep his balance and any shot he made was likely to be wild.

'Hurry up and shoot so we can climb down,' Barney murmured behind him.

From the corner of his eye Jim saw that the ladder down to the car was three paces away, but he also saw the earth blurring by below. He judged that the ground was relatively soft and coated with scrub.

Twin shots from the hired guns whistled past his ears and that was enough for Jim. He grabbed Barney around the shoulders.

'Forget that,' he shouted. 'Jump!'

CHAPTER 8

Sheriff Price considered the statements he'd spread over his desk.

He'd taken testimonies from everyone who had seen anything of interest near the mayor's office yesterday. As this was the first time for eight years he'd tried to work through an investigation on his own, he'd been surprised by how much he'd enjoyed the challenge. He was even whistling to himself now that he was close to deciding upon the sequence of events.

It all appeared to have happened as Mayor Nixon had said it had, but there were anomalies.

One man had seen Nixon leave his office, but he had been sure that that was later in the day. When Price had traced the man's movements he had confirmed he must have been seen after Barney Dale had left town. Another man had heard a commotion in the mayor's office but, again, after Barney had left town.

Then there was Barney Dale himself. Whenever Price considered him he was sure of one thing: Barney wasn't a murderer.

Before Mayor Nixon had come to town and Price had been Sheriff Martin Overton's deputy, he'd had instincts that could spot a killer. That residue of the man he'd once been said that Barney couldn't have killed Sherman Donner.

If caught stealing, Barney would have tried to talk Sherman into believing he was putting the money somewhere safe, or some such tall tale, but he wouldn't have killed him. Price had spent a week looking after him and he always got to know the man on the other side of the bars.

That thought made Price consider Billy Jameson, his only remaining prisoner. He'd convinced himself that Billy was a killer, but two weeks of looking after the young man had told him a different tale. Now he thought him to be just a morose and troubled kid who had yet to find a purpose to his life.

So maybe he wasn't such a good judge of character as he'd thought.

He stood and went over to Billy's cell. As usual Billy was sitting on his cot with his legs pulled up to his chin, staring into space.

'Billy?' he said.

Several second passed before Billy looked up.

'I don't want nothing,' he murmured.

'I wasn't offering. Deputy Carter will be taking over shortly and I wanted to ask you something.'

The mention of Carter made Billy shiver. Carter had been Mayor Nixon's choice for a deputy, a role he'd adopted with enthusiasm after being one of

78

Nixon's hired guns for several years. Carter had ambition and that meant Price trusted him less than he trusted the rest of Nixon's men.

'Go on,' Billy said.

'Did you do it?' Price asked.

This question made Billy show signs of animation for the first time since his arrest. He hurled himself off his cot and in three long paces came up to the bars, making Price back away a pace.

'Why are you asking me that?' he demanded.

Price shrugged, finding that despite the outburst he didn't feel threatened by this young man.

'Because while you're awaiting trial, I still have to consider other possibilities,' he said, having decided this answer would sound better than that he was wondering how good a judge of character he was. 'So I want to hear what happened again to get my thoughts straight.'

Billy considered him, then sighed and gave a slow nod.

'My story hasn't changed. I was angry because Orson Brown wasn't going to pay me.' Billy's eyes glazed as he recalled the events. 'He paced back and forth shouting at me. Then there was a loud bang and he stumbled.'

'The gunshot?'

'I realized it was that afterwards, but at the time I thought he'd knocked something over. I wasn't paying attention. I'd been getting told off a lot.'

'I can imagine.'

'Then I saw the blood and I went to him, but I

79

couldn't do anything. Then my . . . Jim McGuire came in and then you. You saw the rest.'

'Were you holding a gun?'

'No. Jim taught me how to use one, but I wasn't carrying a gun and neither was Orson.'

Price cast his mind back to those events. His own recollection, which he'd detailed in his statement, was that Billy had been brandishing a gun. Nobody else had seen that gun, admittedly, but neither had anyone but Jim been sure he hadn't held a gun.

'And can you prove your claim that someone came in the back door and shot him?'

'That's not my claim. Jim said he saw the open door. I never noticed that.'

Price sighed. Even if he didn't believe Billy about the gun, he'd heard enough prisoners tell lies to know that the more desperate their position, the more desperate their lies. Yet Billy had never tried to spin a tale about any other killer, something that implied he was telling the truth, no matter how unlikely that was.

'And so you ran, hoping to catch the killer?'

'Maybe I did, maybe I didn't,' Billy said, shrugging. 'I can't remember. I was scared and shocked. I just ran.'

'Until Deputy Carter and Hector Pike arrested you and despite your innocence you put up one hell of a fight to avoid capture.'

'So Deputy Carter claimed,' Billy snapped, then gulped, his gaze darting up to look over Price's shoulder.

The door creaked, then footfalls sounded, making

Price turn to see that Deputy Carter had arrived to look after the law office.

'I claimed what?' Carter asked.

Sheriff Price gulped when he realized that Carter might have overheard what he'd been discussing with Billy.

'That you'd feed him a good meal this evening,' he said, covering up their conversation before Billy could reply.

'I never said I'd do that,' Carter muttered.

'More lies,' Price said. He turned to Billy and conveyed with raised eyebrows that he should say nothing and that they would speak later about their interrupted conversation.

'That's all that one knows how to do.' Carter paced over to Price's desk and glared down at the statements. 'What's all this trash?'

'It's the evidence that'll prove what Barney Dale did,' Price said, moving over to join Carter.

'And what did he do?'

'Nixon's story is what happened.'

'Of course it was,' Carter said, picking up the nearest sheet. 'Why did you bother?'

'For the trial, so put that down.' Price reached for the paper. 'They're in the right order to prove what happened.'

'A trial?' With a mocking gleam in his eye Carter held the paper away from Price's outstretched hand until he stopped trying to take it. 'Are you being serious?'

'I don't know what you mean. Jim McGuire will

bring Barney back and—'

'You're a fool, Price, an utter fool.' Carter threw the paper to the desk, his eyes wide and his teeth bared in an exaggerated sneer. 'Why did an idiot like you think he could ever be a lawman?'

Price heard the contempt in the question, but he answered honestly.

'Ten years ago I became Sheriff Martin Overton's deputy, and I was a good one at that. We didn't even have a mayor back in those days. Then Jake Nixon came along and Overton got shot. . . .' Price trailed off and sighed. Carter didn't want to hear the story of how he'd become Mayor Nixon's puppet. 'I'll leave. I've got a town to patrol.'

'You do that, Sheriff.' Carter snorted with contempt. 'Go and keep the peace and make sure the townsfolk of White Ridge feel safe and sound in their beds.'

Through the flickering flames of the campfire Jim considered his new companion Barney Dale, wondering, as he had done during the few moments they'd rested today, whether he could trust him.

Throughout their escape from the train and their hurried passage from the tracks to a point of safety, Barney had given him no further information to persuade him to believe his story.

In his former life Jim had tracked down many men like Barney and knew that, in Barney's position, he would say anything to save his life, but in this case he was inclined to believe Barney. Pike and Hyde had been determined to kill Barney on sight and they did have instructions from Mayor Nixon that they weren't prepared to voice.

Even if his concerns were misplaced, the fact that Nixon had claimed Barney was guilty probably meant that more had taken place in his office than he'd admitted. At the very least, Jim had concluded, he had to ensure Barney reached White Ridge safely.

'It appears we've got away from Nixon's hired guns,' he said, deciding to tackle that issue now. 'But I know one thing for sure: they won't give up. So we have to discuss how we're going to get back to White Ridge.'

'The next few days will be mighty dangerous,' Barney said, rising to his feet. 'So you decide what to do. I've got business elsewhere.'

'Where are you going?' Jim demanded.

Barney pointed to the side of the large overhanging rock beneath which they'd sought safety for the night.

'To find some bushes.'

'You don't leave my sight.'

'Then come with me or let me do it here, but I can assure you, I ain't doing nothing you'll want to see.'

Barney moved to undo his belt and squat, and so with a raised hand Jim acknowledged that Barney could have privacy. Barney hurried away, but the moment he was out of his sight Jim stood and paced around the overhang in the opposite direction to the way Barney had gone.

He climbed to higher ground to look down on the other side of the overhang. At first he couldn't see

Barney in the gloom but then he saw a bush shake, then another.

He was about to head back to the fire, assuming that Barney had been honest with his claim about his intentions, when another bush shook. Then Barney came into view, hunched over and tiptoeing away from the overhang at a furtive pace that suggested he had other things on his mind.

Jim looked ahead to work out Barney's future route, then climbed down from the overhang. Two minutes of hurrying later he was lying on his front in the gathering gloom 200 yards from the overhang, breathing shallowly.

Patiently he waited until he heard grit rasp, then again, the sounds coming nearer. Then Barney came into view, placing his feet to the ground carefully while looking over his shoulder. Jim let Barney enjoy a few more moments of thinking he was getting away before speaking up.

'That's far enough,' he said.

Barney flinched as if shot, then swung round.

'I was looking for the right place to—'

'Save your breath. Your reputation precedes you.'

Barney placed his hands on his hips, gathering his composure with a deep breath.

'Then I'll save my breath.'

'You'll need it. We're a day's ride from White Ridge, without horses. It'll be a slow and dangerous trek and we need to work together.'

'If White Ridge is over there,' Barney said, swinging his hand overarm and pointing in the opposite direction, 'I'm going that way.'

Barney raised his eyebrows, smiled, then did a double take and hurtled off into the night in the direction he'd indicated.

Jim watched his receding figure, sighing to himself. Then, seeing no choice, he set off after him, but he conserved his strength and kept up a steady pace. At first Barney got a one-hundred-yard lead on him but his pace rapidly fell away and after another hundred yards he was staggering, waving his arms and running doubled over.

As Barney slowed to almost a walking pace Jim caught up with him easily. But since he showed no sign of stopping his foolhardy dash into the night Jim threw himself at him, grabbed him around the waist and knocked him to the ground.

The two men went sprawling and when Jim rolled off him Barney just lay on his front, wheezing in great gasps of air. Jim got to his feet and placed a hand on Barney's shoulder to usher him back to the overhang.

'That sure was stupid,' he said.

'But I don't want to die,' Barney whined.

'You won't.' Jim patted his holster. 'I've done this sort of thing before. I'll get you to a court of law.'

Barney rolled to a sitting position still breathing heavily, then sighed and heaved himself to his feet to consider Jim. He got his breathing under control with several huge gasps.

'I don't suppose there's anything I can say that'll persuade you not to go to White Ridge, is there?'

'Nope.'

'Because of Billy Jameson?'

'That's part of it.'

Barney considered, then nodded. 'That mean you did a deal with Nixon to find me in return for him helping Billy?'

Jim smiled on hearing this perceptive comment.

'I did, but I've decided to believe your story. If Nixon was behind Sherman's murder, I reckon he was also determined to have Billy charged, because he was involved in Orson Brown's murder too.' Jim pointed to the overhang, inviting Barney to walk with him. 'I intend to get you to White Ridge and then we'll see what the truth drags out.'

Barney started walking back to the overhang at a slow pace, his head lowered. When he spoke again his voice was low and resigned.

'I spent time with Billy in the jailhouse. He's a good kid. I'd hate to see him suffer, so if you want to help him, then that's—'

'That's enough talk,' Jim snapped, putting on an aggrieved tone that covered the amusement he felt at Barney's weak attempt at subterfuge. 'I've heard all the stories. You won't fool me by claiming you've been so overcome by Billy's plight you'll go back to White Ridge voluntarily.'

Barney's thin smile suggested that his plan had been to sow the seeds of an apparent change of heart that would lull Jim into a false sense of security. He didn't speak again until they were back beside the fire, and when he did his tone was quick and determined and his gaze firm in the reflected firelight.

'Then I'll tell you the truth, Jim,' he said. 'Billy can take his own chances. I care only about myself, so I'll continue to try to escape any chance I get, not because I'm afraid of what a court might do to me, but because I'm innocent and a powerful man ain't. That means I'm a dead man unless I can find a way out of this, and it'll be my own way.'

'Obliged for your honesty, but after what you saw in the mayor's office and with the kind of men who are after you, you're a dead man if you don't have my protection. So think about this: if I spend all my time watching you, I won't be spending that time watching out for the people who are after you. You'll end up dead even quicker.'

Barney lowered his head and stared into the flames, his stooped shoulders suggesting that this viewpoint had had the desired effect.

'All right,' he said. 'I'll give you this: I won't give you no trouble while you're protecting me, but if I see a better chance to get out of this alive, I'll take it.'

'I accept your terms,' Jim said, although he hadn't believed the declaration. 'So this is what we'll do. We'll rest up tonight. Then tomorrow we'll set off for White Ridge on foot.'

Barney nodded, then spread his hands to display his padded jacket.

'On foot won't be necessary,' he said, smiling. 'If we're a team, I'll find a way to use this money and make our journey a little more pleasant.'

CHAPTER 9

Barney Dale peered through the crack between two crates at the small expanse of visible sky. He sighed, then shuffled round to face Jim, who was stretching his cramped limbs.

'When I said I'd buy us a way to White Ridge that was more pleasant than being on foot,' he said, 'I didn't have this in mind.'

'I know,' Jim said, 'that's why I chose it. I want us to arrive in White Ridge unseen.'

'And sore, numb, and all cramped up,' Barney grumbled, shifting position again.

Jim smiled in sympathy even if he didn't regret his decision.

This morning on foot they had made their way towards White Ridge, taking a course that ran parallel to the railroad tracks. Around noon they had found a homestead where Barney had bartered to buy a horse, a mangy and bow-backed bay. Luckily, they'd been saved from the indignity of negotiating for its dubious assistance by the arrival of Dave Hallow, a trader.

For twenty dollars they'd bought passage to White Ridge on the back of his provision-laden wagon. It was a journey that would take the rest of the day and which, as they had been moving to higher ground over the last few hours, Jim reckoned was a few hours from completion.

He was also growing in confidence that they could reach town while avoiding Pike, Hyde, and anyone else who might be looking for them. But he wasn't so confident as not to hide among the crates of provisions and sacks of corn on the back of the wagon.

Through the gaps he could see the ridge that gave White Ridge its name to their side, its light-coloured rocks gleaming in the rays from the lowering sun. The river that ran to the north of White Ridge was roaring by somewhere below and their slow progress suggested the route they were on was a high and treacherous one.

Barney was searching for a new reason to grumble when for the first time this day Jim heard an untoward noise. Barney fell silent and both men strained their hearing.

'Move aside,' Dave shouted from the driver's seat ahead. 'The wagon's too wide for all your horses, unless you want to end up in the river.'

'We'll move aside,' a strident voice called out, 'when you've answered a question.'

On the back of the wagon Barney and Jim looked at each other, silently asking the other whether they recognized the voice. Neither of them did but that didn't dispel Jim's feeling of foreboding.

'Then ask it,' Dave said, drawing the wagon to a halt. 'I've got a delivery to make in White Ridge.'

'That mean you've come from Milton Creek?' An affirmative grunt sounded. 'Have you seen anyone acting strangely today?'

This made Jim wince then shift his weight to draw his gun.

'I see plenty of strange things out on the trail. I could tell you some stories. Why only yesterday I saw a—'

'Spare me the wild and pointless tale. I mean two men on foot.'

Long moments passed in which Jim could picture Dave rubbing his jaw and ruminating, as he had when they'd negotiated for passage and he'd realized they had money.

'Now I might have done and I might not have done,' he drawled. 'My memory ain't what it used to be.'

Jim glanced at Barney.

'He's selling us out,' he whispered.

'He's not,' Barney said. 'A straight no would appear suspicious. He's talking us out of a tricky situation.'

'Then let's hope he's better at it than you are.'

Barney narrowed his eyes in irritation, then cocked his head when one of the new arrivals spoke up again.

'We ain't paying for information. Either tell us what you've seen or we'll tip your wagon down into the river.'

'No need to get uppity. I can defend myself.'

'Too late!' another voice said.

90

Dave uttered a strangulated gasp after which there was silence for several seconds. On the back of the wagon Barney mouthed a question as to what was happening. Jim mouthed back that the situation was turning ugly, then patted his gun.

Barney got the idea and did his best to burrow down into the base of the wagon as outside slow hoof-beats approached.

Then, closer to the wagon, an uncompromising demand rang out.

'One wrong move and I fire!'

Jim winced and glanced at Barney.

'Pike,' he mouthed. Then he moved away from Barney to get closer to the front of the wagon, his next actions now unavoidable.

'What's wrong?' Dave asked.

'Maybe nothing, but we'll find out soon enough. Get down off that wagon. Then we'll search your wares. If we don't find anything interesting, you can move on to White Ridge.'

'And if we do,' another voice said, clearly Hyde's, 'you'll follow your wagon down into the river.'

Jim made a calming gesture, telling Barney to stay where he was. Then he examined the stacked heaps of produce. There were two barrels with an empty sack draped over them, then four crates piled in a block were between him and the seat. He slipped in between the barrels and placed a hand on the sack, ready to toss it aside at the right moment.

If he was to get them out of this situation alive, he couldn't avoid meting out death, he accepted, but he consoled himself with the thought that, unlike the last time he'd killed, this time he didn't have a choice.

'I don't want no trouble,' Dave said, his tone low and serious. 'I ain't seen no men since I left Milton Creek, so if you want to waste your time searching every barrel and crate back there, do it. Just pay me for any damage and if any of that damage is to Nixon's goods, you can explain what you did to him.'

Jim knelt in a poised position, hoping Dave's bluff would work. Long moments passed in silence until Pike spoke up.

'We'll do just that,' he said. 'You, search the wagon.'

'That's your choice,' Dave said. 'I've—'

A rifle shot tore out, closely followed by another gunshot. Then the seat creaked and the thud of a body hitting wood sounded. Guessing what had happened, Jim threw back the sack and sprang to his feet.

As he rose to his full height the crates came up to his midriff, letting him see the scene. It was pretty much as he'd envisaged. The wagon was on a thin trail winding along the side of the ridge. A steep upward slope was to the right and a precipitous slope down to the distant river was to the left.

Men, presumably hired in Milton Creek, led by Pike and Hyde were positioned before and behind the wagon. Jim's quick glance counted nine men with one man moving to climb up on to the driver's seat from which Dave's body was falling.

Jim turned his gun on that man, blasting him in the chest and throwing him backwards. Two more crisp shots spat out from his gun, sending the only two riders in front of the wagon tumbling from their horses.

Then Jim vaulted the crates to land square on the seat. As he went to one knee he noted that none of the men he'd shot was the leader of the group. But that wasn't as important as the fact that nobody was left on the trail stretching before him other than the two riderless horses.

Jim crouched down, keeping his body below the level of the wares stored on the back of the wagon. He lunged for the reins, but before he reached them lead scythed across his forearm. A bolt of pain ripped through his arm.

He'd taken bullets before and he steeled himself for the all-consuming pain to come, but when he looked at his arm, he saw that he'd been lucky. The bullet had only grazed flesh and he could still open and close his fist.

He raised himself up and fired blind over the tops of the crates, then reloaded and kept low as the return gunfire blasted out. He waited until it had ended, then moved to rise, but before he could fire, another volley sounded and a moment later Barney bounded over the crates to land at his side.

'I told you to stay hidden,' Jim said.

'With them moving in it was getting mighty tough to stay put,' Barney said. 'I figured it was time to tell you to stop sitting around admiring the view and get us the hell out of here.'

Jim gave an appreciative laugh, then pointed at the reins.

'On the count of three, go for 'em and get us moving.'

Jim looked at Barney for long enough to confirm he'd understood, then counted to three quickly and bobbed up. This time he edged over the top of the crates, to see that the remaining six riders were moving purposefully towards the wagon from all directions.

He fired at the nearest man to the side, judging him to be the man who had been keeping him pinned down. His shot flew wide, letting that man and two others return fire.

Splinters flew from the top of the crate as Jim ducked. He stayed down and jerked up again, firing quickly and wildly, but despite his lack of success, he provided enough of a distraction for Barney to take the reins.

With a loud bellow and a crack of his hand, Barney got the wagon moving, the wheels turning slowly then building up speed as they went trundling along the thin trail. Both men kept their heads down as bullets whined overhead or holed the crates and splattered chunks of wood at their backs.

The trail was wide enough for a single rider to pass on either side of them. So Jim kept his gun trained on one side then the other, waiting for someone to risk trying to get ahead of them.

But they covered the first fifty yards then one hundred, without anyone risking it. By then they were rocking their way along faster than Dave would have allowed them to travel this high up.

About 300 yards ahead the trail followed the contours of the ridge before turning sharply to the right. The trail then disappeared from view. They'd have to slow to negotiate that bend and Jim judged that that was where their pursuers would make their move.

He pointed, drawing Barney's attention to the bend, then heard a rattling noise from behind as a shadow passed over him. He turned to see Hyde had leapt on to the wagon and was clambering on to the top of the crates ready to assault them. The wagon was rocking so much that Hyde was struggling to keep his balance, but on seeing that his attempt to sneak up on them unnoticed had failed he swung his gun arm round towards Barney.

With only seconds to react Jim threw his forearm up, blocking Hyde's arm before he could aim. In frustration Hyde squeezed out a shot. The bullet whined a foot over Barney's lowered head, confirming that his main objective was still to silence him.

From his elevated position Hyde bore down on Jim with all his weight, lowering his arm and inching the gun closer and closer to the point where he would be able to shoot Barney.

Jim strained to hold back the descending arm. He couldn't, so in a moment he changed tactics. He stopped resisting and jerked his hand to the side to grab Hyde's jacket, then dropped, yanking down with all his might.

The sudden movement caught Hyde off guard and pulled him forward from the crates. He somersaulted once to land on his back on the seat with his legs thrust high and waving like those of an upturned beetle.

His gun came loose and skittered along the seat, but Jim gave him no time to recover his wits and reach it. He threw himself on to Hyde's chest, grabbing for his shoulder to hold him down with his left hand while swinging his own gun round, aiming to thrust it up under Hyde's chin.

Hyde's eyes opened wide as he saw the gun close on him. He scrambled for purchase, managing to get his feet on to the seat and with a firm kick he forced his way backwards and nearer to the edge, loosening Jim's grip.

'Get him over the side,' Barney shouted from behind Jim.

'I'm trying,' Jim grunted, the bouncing of the wagon over the rocky trail making him struggle to direct the gun in towards Hyde's body.

Then the speeding wagon hurtled over a large rock. A wheel bucked and the rigging and timbers in the base of the wagon protested so loudly that Jim thought the whole wagon would split in two.

Jim felt himself thrust up into the air before he came crashing down again on to the seat. Worse, the jolt gave Hyde the momentum to lever himself to a sitting position and throw himself at Jim. The two men tumbled backwards, knocking into Barney and sending him sliding across the seat.

'Hey,' Barney shouted. 'The reins.'

From the corner of his eye, Jim saw the reins fluttering free, but he put that from his mind as Hyde pressed against him. His arms wrapped around Jim's chest and he strained, aiming to throw him from the wagon. Jim slid towards the edge but then realized he still had a grip of his gun and so with a deft nudge of the wrist he twisted the gun into Hyde's chest, then fired.

At point-blank range the sound was deafening, sending a hot flash across the back of Jim's hand, but he also saw Hyde's eyes glaze with pain before he slipped away to fall from the seat.

'Got him,' Jim said, turning to help Barney regain the reins.

'Too late,' Barney murmured, his pointing and shaking finger making Jim turn, then flinch back in shock.

He had forgotten about the tight bend. It was now just thirty yards ahead and Barney had no control of the horses. They were slowing and surely they wouldn't be so frightened by the gunfire as to carry straight on, but he still leaned forward and lunged for the reins.

While Barney searched for the wheel brake, he grabbed a trailing end then looped it around his wrist to get a firm grip.

'Whoa!' he shouted, dragging back hard, but he was already too late.

The yawning chasm of the slope down to the river was just five yards ahead of the horses. They tore to the side, struggling to escape their rigging, frightened by what lay ahead, but it was too late to slow the wagon's momentum and it carried on inexorably towards the edge.

Timbers snapped and the rigging fell free giving the horses a chance to save themselves, but Jim didn't see whether they took that chance as the wagon reached the edge then tipped over the side.

Below was a long slope, the angle so steep the wagon would struggle to roll down it for more than a few dozen yards.

'Get off!' he shouted, moving to slip over the side, but Barney grabbed his arm before he could leap.

'Staying up here on the high trail is death,' he shouted back.

Jim looked down at the speeding earth below and accepted Barney was right. If jumping didn't kill them, the men up on the trail would.

'All right, but going down there is too,' Jim shouted as the wagon trundled downwards, picking up pace. 'What do you suggest?'

'Hanging on,' Barney shouted. 'And praying!'

Jim slapped Barney's shoulder, then looked back up the slope to see a line of men appear on the edge of the trail to look down at them. As one they raised their guns, took a bead on the departing wagon and fired.

Jim ducked and pushed Barney's head down too, saving them from the lead that tore into the bouncing wagon. But just as every turn of the wheels let them pick up pace it also moved them out of firing range and soon the gunfire was splaying wide.

Jim chose that moment to turn in the seat to return fire but the shaking of the wagon was too great for him to take steady aim. After a few poorly directed shots, he concentrated on holding on to the seat as they barrelled down the slope, the wagon kicking up a huge cloud of dust, the river approaching fast.

'You must be praying hard,' Jim shouted over the cracking and grinding of the wagon. 'It looks as if we might reach the river.'

'And then what?' Barney shouted. 'At this speed we don't stand a chance.'

'We'll worry about that if—' Jim broke off with a screech when a solid object slapped him on the back of the head.

His hand came up in an involuntary reaction to find that a sack of corn had shaken loose from the back of the wagon and had now propped itself against his head. He batted it aside but that only freed the produce behind it to lurch forward. Barrels and crates and sacks came cascading down on him.

Jim pushed the first wave aside but they kept on coming and he felt himself pushed off the seat. He threw up his hands to cushion what was sure to be a bone-breaking fall but then a firm hand slapped down on his back halting his progress.

With Barney holding him up he lay sprawled half-off the seat, looking down at the ground blurring along below just inches from his face. Then Barney tugged, a fortuitously timed bounce over a rock aiding him in dragging Jim back on to the seat.

Jim grabbed a firm hold of the seat to steady himself and nodded his thanks to Barney, but Barney shook his head and pointed.

99

Jim swirled round to look ahead. The river was now just yards away.

'You remember what you said to me yesterday?' Barney said.

'What?' Jim murmured, still disorientated.

'Jump!' Barney shouted.

Jim didn't need a second warning and as the wagon reached the river's edge he hurled himself to the side. He somersaulted once before he hit the water on his back as beside him the wagon slewed into the river with a huge splash.

Under water and winded Jim fought to reach the surface, suffering a few moments of stunned silence before he broke through to the air.

In the choppy waters he floundered as in front of him Barney fought to stay above water. The strong current also took them out from the side as piece by piece Dave's produce and wrecked sections of the broken wagon floated to the surface. When a particularly wide plank bobbed up, Jim put his dwindling strength into making firm strokes towards it.

Three powerful lunges got him to the plank, where he rested his arms over the makeshift raft. With it supporting his weight he relaxed and let the current take him. A few moments later Barney joined him.

'How do we get to the side?' Barney shouted.

'Ain't sure we should do that,' Jim said, jerking his head towards the high trail, which was now receding from view. 'We're moving away from Pike and the others.'

'Get shot or get drowned,' Barney mused. 'Ain't

much of a choice.'

'For now I'll settle for being alive and besides, we're heading downriver and that means we're getting closer to White Ridge.'

'We are, aren't we?' Barney said, brightening.

Jim noted Barney's unexpected pleasure at that thought before he concentrated on staying above water as the current swirled them off into the gathering gloom.

CHAPTER 10

Although Mayor Nixon had said that a growing town like White Ridge needed a newspaper, as yet he'd failed to find an editor he approved of, so the newspaper office was still boarded up.

Sheriff Price stood on the boardwalk outside, wondering if he should try to find a way in. It was clear from Deputy Carter's attitude that Nixon thought he had pushed his luck by quizzing so many witnesses. But the facts surrounding Sherman Donner's murder made less sense the more he thought about them.

Now he was getting a feeling that the same might be true in the case of the earlier murder of Orson Brown, and an old and rarely heeded instinct told him they could even be connected. Unfortunately, it was also clear that Nixon was pleased with his initial assertions of Billy's guilt, so carrying on an investigation would annoy him.

Price shivered at the thought, his movement breaking him out of his reverie and making him realize he'd been standing in front of the office for several minutes. A group of men was looking at him oddly with that mixture of contempt and pity he always saw in people's eyes these days.

To avoid making an immediate decision he made his way round to the back of the office. He found that the back door had also been boarded up, but only two boards covered the framework.

Idly, as if he were just checking that it was secure he tugged on the topmost board. He told himself that if it was firm he'd leave, but the board came away. So, with a sigh, he admitted that this had committed him.

The second board required more tugging, but it still came away from the frame cleanly. Then, before anyone might happen to see him, he slipped inside the darkened interior.

He stood before the door, noting what Orson's killer would have seen if he had stood here. Most of the office was visible but not the part where Orson had fallen.

He paced forward, looking for the moment when that area came into view, but he had to cover ten paces before that happened and he judged that Billy ought to have been able to hear someone moving that far.

Feeling more confident now that he hadn't made a mistake in his judgement of the situation he walked to the area of stained wood where Orson had breathed his last.

He turned and conjured up an image of Billy kneeling beside the body. Again, he thought that he had seen a gun, but when he moved off he noted that several metallic objects were lying around the office.

What their function might be he didn't like to guess.

One such piece caught his eye, lying on the floor as if discarded. It was a short length of metal with a flattened end, which Orson used to align blocks of text.

Price picked it up and ran it through his hands. Perhaps Billy had been holding this when Orson had died, he conjectured. He had been working here, after all. Or maybe Orson had held it.

Then another more distant memory came to him of Orson pacing back and forth, talking through a story for the paper. He had been punctuating his points by slapping the metal length into his other hand.

And Billy had said Orson was pacing.

In a rush he saw the situation in a different light: Orson pacing back and forth with the metal object in his hand, then getting shot from the back door and taking a few stumbling paces before he fell. The shocked Billy ran to his side, knelt, picked up the length of metal, holding it as if it were a gun. . . .

'Perhaps Billy Jameson didn't kill Orson Brown, after all,' he said to himself, 'and perhaps Barney Dale didn't kill Sherman Donner either.'

Now sure that he'd learned something vital he left the office. He used the metal to hammer in the nails and replace the boards. Then he tucked the metal length into his pocket and turned to leave.

But while he'd been working three people had arrived silently: Mayor Nixon and two of his hired guns.

'What were you doing in there?' Nixon demanded.

'I was looking around,' Price said with an audible

gulp in his drying throat. 'A trial will be coming up and I thought I ought to refresh my memory.'

'Did I tell you to do that?' Nixon paused, although his glaring eyes suggested he didn't want an answer. 'I didn't. Neither did I tell you to bother people with your pointless questions about what happened in my office two days ago.'

'But there will be trials for both cases and—'

'There will be, but they have nothing to do with you. You got it right about Billy two weeks ago and as for Barney Dale. . . .' Nixon leaned forward. 'You've spent enough time on him. Go back to doing what you usually do. Parade up and down the boardwalk behind your shiny star while my men take care of the law in White Ridge.'

'I can't do that,' Price said, surprising himself with the audacity of his response and the confidence in his tone. 'I don't mind you helping me out when the guilty get dealt with, but I'm not sure yet that you got it right this time.'

Even Nixon's usually unresponsive hired guns winced at that comment, and so they should have. Price reckoned he'd never spoken such defiance before and it must have shocked Nixon too, as he took several seconds to find his voice. When he did he paced up to stand toe to toe with the sheriff.

'I am helping you?' he intoned, barking out every word. 'And I, who have run this town for the last eight years, got it wrong, and you, who's only fit to slop out prisoners, got it right?'

'What I said probably didn't come out well,' Price

mumbled. 'What I meant was—'

'I don't care what you meant! Your role isn't to think or say or do anything anyone cares about. The only reason I've tolerated you is because nobody with any self-respect could do what you do. The moment you start getting ideas, I'll replace you with someone who knows his place, like Deputy Carter.'

'You can't. I got re-elected last month for another term.'

'And so did your predecessor and you know what happened to him.'

Nixon's right eye twitched before he glanced away. Price had never considered that anything had happened to his old mentor Sheriff Martin Overton other than he'd got shot in the line of duty. But he considered it now.

When Nixon looked back at him Price saw in his narrowed eyes an acknowledgement that while he'd been angry he'd revealed more than he should have.

'I'm sorry,' Price said, his bowels turning to ice as he accepted that he was perhaps seconds away from suffering the same fate as Overton. 'I was just doing what I thought you wanted me to do.'

Nixon sneered. 'I liked you better when you were drinking, Price. Then you didn't waste my time by thinking. Now you need to know what happens when you do.'

He gave a quick gesture to the hired guns and turned away. Price moved to follow him but a hired gun threw out an arm, blocking his way. Price turned the other way, but found that the other gun was blocking his way too.

This man gave him a resigned shrug that said that what was about to happen wasn't personal, then thundered a low punch deep into Price's guts that had him folding over, coughing and gasping in pain.

A bunched blow on the back of his neck sent him to his knees before a contemptuous light kick tipped him over on to his back. He lay, knowing fighting back would get him only a worse beating and hoping that those blows would be enough to satisfy Nixon, but they hadn't finished with him yet.

The second man dragged him to his feet and delivered another swinging blow to his ribs that sent him to the ground again, whereupon he was raised up and knocked down again. Price tried to roll with the punches while he waited for the men to tire or to decide they'd given him enough of a warning.

But the men seemed incapable of tiring and they went about their task with grim determination.

He consoled himself with the realization that they were avoiding hitting his face, presumably to ensure that nobody would see any outward sign of his beating, so at least that meant he still had a second chance to redeem himself.

His life contracted into a steady rhythm of punch, pain, falling, being pulled back to his feet, punch, pain . . . and so it was with some surprise that when he tensed himself for the next blow it didn't come.

Through pained eyes he watched the hired guns walking away, neither man having said a word throughout the beating, but even though the next punch wouldn't come Price still fell over to land on his side.

How long he lay there he didn't know as his concentration remained fixed on the small patch of dirt before his face.

Part of him wanted to defy Nixon and continue investigating the murders until he uncovered the truth, especially as he knew why Nixon didn't want him to pry. Eight years ago Nixon had had Sheriff Overton killed. He had been a good man whom Price had trusted and admired, and that meant Nixon had probably been behind the other recent murders too.

But the larger part of him never wanted to be in pain again, especially as that beating had been just a warning. What would come later if he persisted would be far worse.

His mind remained blank, perhaps refusing to consider his dilemma for fear of what it might decide until eventually he started to wonder whether he should head back to the law office and inspect the damage. But he felt so numbed he couldn't make himself stand up and instead he curled up into a ball. He wished he could stay here until he quietly died and didn't have to face any problems ever again.

He could have stayed there until sleep claimed him, but he heard slow footfalls approaching. Feeling worried that Nixon had returned he shook himself out of his cataleptic torpor and looked up.

He saw black boots and raised his gaze to consider the black-clad man who wore them. Only when his gaze reached the face did he recognize Isaiah Jones,

Nixon's enigmatic rival.

Isaiah contemplated him, his face a blank mask, then he reached down, stopping with his hand inches from Price's wrist. Price stared at the hand without understanding. Only when Isaiah withdrew the hand, then thrust it out again, did he realize what his intention was.

He grabbed the hand and let Isaiah pull him to his feet where he stood stooped.

'Obliged for your help,' he said, rubbing his ribs.

'And I'm obliged for yours,' Isaiah said. He patted Price on the shoulder, making him wince. 'You're doing a mighty fine job, Sheriff, a mighty fine job indeed.'

With that comment he turned away and headed off. Price watched him leave, bemused but uncomprehending as to what that odd encounter had meant. Then he made his slow way round the newspaper office.

By the time he arrived on the main road Isaiah was nowhere to be seen but at least meeting him had taken his mind off his pains and had helped him to get moving. Standing as tall as he could in case anyone saw him he walked to the law office.

Walking straight helped to free some of the tightness in his chest and limbs, but what he saw when he arrived in the office made him stumble. Carter wasn't there but all the statements he'd painstakingly collected and collated had been torn into strips and stomped into the floor around his desk.

The desk itself was clear except for a whiskey bottle

and a glass standing gleaming in the centre. He hadn't had whiskey in the office for two years and he'd never seen Carter drink while on duty. Someone must have left it for him.

Price paced over to the desk and flopped down onto his chair. He checked his top drawer, but confirmed that all the evidence that detailed the anomalies in Nixon's story had gone. Worse, he was sure that if he tried to requestion anyone, it would be the last thing he did. There was no way he could prove. . . .

The weight in his pocket attracted his attention so he drew out the short length of metal. He threw it from hand to hand then placed it on the desk and nodded to himself, accepting that here at least was proof of Billy's innocence, if not of someone else's guilt.

That meant there were still things he could do, if he dared.

He considered the bottle, knowing that the madness of defying Nixon and investigating and perhaps even proving he was a murderer was more frightening than handing himself over to the welcoming smoothness of the whiskey. He picked up the bottle, held it in his grasp for the first time for two years, then reached for the glass with the other hand.

Neither hand was shaking as they always had done when he drank.

'I'm doing a mighty fine job,' he said to himself, recalling Isaiah's words. 'I must be if one man thinks I am.'

And that decided it.

He hurled the glass at the wall, watching it smash into fragments, then hurled the bottle after it.

Whiskey fumes filled the office, tickling his nostrils while the noise made Billy rush to the bars. Price breathed in the pungent fumes, then turned to him.

'You know something, Billy?' he said. 'That whiskey just don't smell right.'

CHAPTER 11

'You dry yet?' Barney asked, feeling the discarded clothes he'd draped over a branch.

'Dry enough,' Jim said. He broke off from his task of steadily reassembling his dried gun to pat his own pile of clothes, then his vest front. 'What about you?'

'I am, but it's these bills I'm worried about.'

Jim almost offered a sarcastic reply, but Barney's money had got them most of the way to White Ridge in good time. So he contented himself with smiling as Barney padded around in his underclothes, carrying out the tricky task of drying out wads of wet bills before the fire in a way that ensured they didn't burst into flame.

So far he'd lost only a few strays that had peeled away and wafted off into the flames, but the experience had helped Barney work out a safe method. Now he'd weighted each wad down with a stone and placed it near to the fire. Every few minutes he monitored each wad in rotation, to ensure that none of them was getting scorched.

They were some distance downriver from the scene of their frenzied plummeting from the high trail. How far they'd floated they weren't sure, as they'd spent most of their journey trying to stay above water and reach the side. When they'd eventually dragged themselves on to dry land, darkness had descended and they'd had no choice but to make a fire or freeze.

They'd counted themselves lucky in surviving the plunge into the water and even luckier that they'd reached land at a point where the ridge to their side formed a ravine so precipitous that approaching them would be difficult.

'Let's hope you can find a way to use that money tomorrow,' Jim said. He hefted his gun, considering it now cleaned after the soaking they'd had and placed it on the neat pile of his dried jacket and shirt.

'I will. It's what I'm best at. You just concentrate on what you're best at.' Barney reflected on their situation. 'And you did well back there. From what Billy had said about you, I didn't take you to be someone who could shoot and fight like that.'

'You did well too,' Jim said in all honesty.

He had expected Barney to take the first opportunity to escape that came along, and the confusion back in the wagon and in the water had offered several chances. But Barney had stayed with him and they'd even helped each other several times.

'Obliged,' Barney said. 'But now that we know the kind of opposition we're facing you have to be open with me. Can you seriously take on all of Nixon's men?'

113

'I can. Trust me.'

'I'm trying to, but I don't know you.'

Jim patted the gun, then stood and paced closer to the fire to warm his hands.

'All you need to know is I'm the kind of man who can get you to White Ridge, keep you alive, and take on Nixon.'

'And Jim McGuire, quiet man, and guardian of a wrongly convicted prisoner can do that, can he?'

Barney was fishing for details about his life and Jim couldn't blame him. When the few people who had done that before had become too personal he had always veered the conversation away from the uncomfortable subject of his past. But Barney was clearly concerned about putting his life in his hands. As he needed to keep his attention on the dangers they would face and not on keeping Barney an effective prisoner, he decided to talk to someone about his situation for the first time.

'I used to be a manhunter,' he said, looking into the flames, 'perhaps the finest. I hung up my gun though and settled down in White Ridge. I vowed that I'd never pick up that gun again, but needing to get Billy freed from jail has made me break that vow. And as getting you to White Ridge will help Billy, know this: I will get you there.'

Barney nodded. 'What made you hang up your gun?'

'You don't want to know that.'

Barney considered this before he replied:

'Then don't tell me, but the problem I have is I'm

114

torn between whether you or my own wits represent my best chance of surviving.' Barney pointed at Jim, then at the drying money before he tapped his forehead. 'Knowing who you are and what happened to you might clarify my thinking.'

Jim considered Barney's request, recalling that earlier this evening in the water Barney had appeared more accepting of his need to return to White Ridge. He gave a non-committed shrug and moved forward to poke the flames with a stick.

The sudden burst of heat made Barney bleat and drag several wads of bills back a few paces. Jim laughed at his dismay, helping to allay his concern about talking, and the friendly laugh Barney returned convinced him that in this case it would do them both good to talk.

'I ain't never told anyone this,' he said, 'so know that I'm trusting you plenty by talking.'

'I may like to talk, but anything you say won't get repeated.'

'Glad to hear it. That'll just stop me having to kill you.' Jim smiled until Barney returned a smile then looked at the fire. 'I'd hunted so many men I couldn't remember all their names no more, but I knew one thing. I'd never failed and I had me the best reputation a man could want. The people who hired Jim McGuire ... Luther Mallory ... had even stopped asking to see a body. They knew that if they gave me the money, the job would be done.'

'And was it?'

'Every time, without fail and without any questions

115

asked, and that was the problem. I'd started out as a bounty hunter with some morals as to the kind of missions I took on, but somewhere along the line I stopped asking questions. So when one day a businessman who'd lost five thousand dollars at the poker-table paid me to kill the man who beat him, I didn't ask for more than a name.'

'When you found him did he take you on and best you?' Barney asked, guessing where this story was leading.

'Nope. I wish he had. It wasn't too hard to find him. A man with a sudden windfall is easy to find.' Jim looked up and winked.

'I know,' Barney murmured with a rueful rub of his chin.

Jim began pacing around now that the tale had reached the part he always tried to avoid thinking about.

'My quarry was travelling with a partner and they'd laid down a trail anyone could have followed. When I caught up with them I targeted the partner. I got talking to him in a saloon and offered him a meal to share when he left town. He agreed and so, a few miles out of town, we sat around a camp-fire, just like we're doing now.'

Barney cringed back with mock fear, then stood up, his downcast and troubled eyes showing his reaction hadn't been entirely false.

'You do know that this tale is supposed to comfort me?' he said after stretching his legs.

'I do, but there's no comfort here. We talked until

my target arrived and he was just what I had expected. He was an ordinary man who'd got lucky while looking for work. Whenever he could he sent money to his family and he'd always dreamed of having enough money to let him go home and repay their faith in him. He even thought I was down on my luck and offered me money to help me out. He was a decent man.'

'So what happened?' Barney asked after Jim had paused for several seconds.

'I shot him. Then I shot his partner.'

Barney recoiled, then spent the next few minutes pottering around unnecessarily checking on the state of his drying bills.

'You shouldn't have done that,' he said at last.

'I know, but I had a job to do and I always finished what I'd started. The partner I killed outright, as I always did, but not the target. Perhaps my conscience veered my aim. I only wounded him.'

'He lived?' Barney looked up with hope in his eyes that this story would have a happy ending. Jim extinguished that hope with a cold glare.

'I stood over him, gun aimed down at his head and with death staring him in the face there was only one thing he wanted to say. Tell my family I'm dead, he said. They deserve to know why the letters have stopped. I nodded. Then I killed him.'

'You have changed since then, haven't you?' Barney asked with an audible gulp before he started nervously pacing back and forth.

Jim matched his pacing on the other side of the fire.

117

'That's the point of my story. I realized then that I'd become a monster. So I collected up his money, raided his saddlebags, and buried him and his partner. Then I set out to write that letter, but I couldn't find the words. I told myself that if I ever hoped to wipe away the memory of what I'd done I'd have to find his family and tell them the truth to their faces, which is what I did.'

'Did they accept it?'

'Nope. His wife had died. He didn't know that, the letters were all one way, but his son was still alive. . . .'

'Ah,' Barney said and stopped walking. 'I see now. Billy Jameson?'

'Yup. I couldn't tell Billy I'd killed his father, but he filled in the details for himself. He thought I was his father's partner . . . Jim McGuire. I didn't dissuade him. I gave him the windfall his father had died for but he didn't want money. He wanted a link with his father. So I tried to make things right, tried to take the place of the man I'd killed. And because Jim had been planning to come to White Ridge to settle down and enjoy his share of the windfall, I came here. The rest you know.'

'Obliged for the truth,' Barney said, his voice gruff with emotion. 'I understand now why helping Billy is so important to you and perhaps why I can trust you to keep me alive.'

'Trust, after hearing that?'

'Yeah. It was an honest tale and it'd take something terrible like that to change a man like you.' Barney raised his eyebrows. 'Provided that completing the

118

mission is something that hasn't changed?'

'It hasn't.'

'Then I put myself in your hands.' Barney came round the fire and held out a hand. 'Get me to White Ridge and I'll speak up against Mayor Nixon and do the best I can for Billy.'

'Obliged to you for accepting my word,' Jim said, taking the hand.

'Obliged to you for trusting me enough to talk.'

Jim patted Barney's shoulder then returned to where he'd been sitting. He got as far as crouching down beside his dried clothes and moving to put them on. . . .

His gun was no longer sitting on his clothes.

He flinched back then swirled round to see the gun was in Barney's hand.

'You double-crossing varmint,' Jim snapped, advancing a pace on Barney.

'Don't come any closer,' Barney ordered, shuffling the gun back into his hand as he aimed it at Jim.

'You lied to me. Got me to reveal all that just so you could get me off guard.'

Barney shrugged and gave Jim a shame-faced look.

'Look at it this way, you let your guard down for someone like me, which means you've softened and you're not the best man to keep me alive.'

Jim scowled. 'I still am that man, despite showing compassion for a liar like you.'

'I didn't lie. I always said if a chance came my way I'd take it.' Barney backed away a pace. 'And I ain't lying when I say this: nobody will ever know your secret. And I really do hope things work out well for Billy.'

'I'm all cut up by that speech.' Jim advanced a long pace on Barney and spread his hands out. 'So you're going to have to shoot me if you don't want to go back to White Ridge.'

'No further,' Barney demanded, stepping back to the edge of the fire, then jerking to the side as the flames licked at his boots.

Jim took another long pace. 'You ain't a killer. You've never needed a gun with that mouth of yours. You won't shoot me.'

'I will!' Barney shouted, taking another pace backwards, but he accidentally kicked a wad of bills sending them flying. Half of the bills headed into the flames, the others fluttered away.

Barney watched in horror as hundreds of dollars flared up before his eyes, the distraction giving Jim enough time to throw himself forward. He hit Barney full in the chest with his right arm thrust upwards to push him backwards and his left arm held sideways to veer the gun hand away from him.

Barney didn't fire, either through being distracted or justifying Jim's gamble that he didn't want to shoot him. Jim ran him backwards for four paces until Barney's legs folded beneath him, sending them both tumbling. The gun skittered away from both of their grasps.

Jim landed on Barney's chest and moved to hold him down, but Barney kicked upwards. He managed to loop his feet around Jim's legs, then pushed hard enough to send Jim rolling towards the fire.

Jim rolled once, then slammed an elbow to the ground to stop his motion, but his elbow jarred against a stone, sending a numbing jolt of pain down his arm. The brief agony eroded the last ounce of good will he had about Barney's reasonableness in not shooting.

He got to his feet, his left arm hanging slackly and paced up to Barney, who must have seen the anger in his eyes, for when he stood he raised his hands in a warding-off gesture.

'Maybe,' he said, 'we should talk about this.'

'You're a man who talks with his mouth.' Jim glanced at his hand. 'I'm a man who talks with his fist.'

He swung back his fist and put all his pent-up annoyance behind a swinging uppercut to Barney's jaw that sent him spinning away. Barney rolled twice before he came to a halt in a crumpled heap.

Jim flexed his fist, then his numbed arm, feeling more relaxed when he found that his arm was working again.

Barney lay for several moments fingering his jaw. Then, slowly, he got to his knees. He looked up at Jim and red-eyed anger had replaced his previously docile demeanour. Admittedly some of the redness came from the firelight, but Jim straightened, then beckoned him on.

Barney uttered a roar of bravado that echoed in the ravine above, then came to his feet, kicking off with such force he launched himself off the ground. With his arms thrust forward and straight he hammered into Jim. The two men went down.

Then, with their arms interlocked, they fought. Kicks, gouges, and short-arm punches were traded back and forth as each man fought for supremacy.

They rolled over and over each other, neither man giving thought to anything other than pummelling the other into the dirt. Barney gave as good as he received and, by the time the red mist had faded from the minds of both, lips were bloody and ribs were bruised, but still they fought on.

How long it could have gone on Jim no longer cared, but he had also lost all sense of where they were when suddenly heat seared along his back. For a frantic moment he wondered what had happened. Then he realized they'd rolled into the fire.

Barney was lying on top of him and he too felt the lick of flame. With a pained roar he kicked himself away, the motion pushing Jim back into the fire. Jim fought to move himself without putting his hands to the ground, but Barney swung back, grabbed his vest front, then yanked him away from the flames.

Then they both rolled around in the dirt, batting out the flames. Jim was the first to extinguish the embers on his underclothes, so he looked out for Barney, seeing him trying to tear off his burning vest.

Jim bounded over to him, slapped a hand on his back, then rapidly slapped at the flames, batting the burning embers to the ground and stamping on them. Then he turned Barney round, checking him over while Barney did the same to him.

When they were sure they weren't about to burst

into flames they considered each other. Barney was bloodied, dirty and red of face, and his vest now consisted of two thin strips of cloth dangling from his shoulders.

Jim laughed and, presumably because he presented the same kind of pitiful sight, Barney laughed too.

'Enough?' Jim asked.

'Enough,' Barney agreed.

'And enough of you trying to talk your way out of going to White Ridge?'

'I'll always do that, but not with you no more.'

'Then if you stick with that promise, a couple of burnt vests and a few bruises was worth it.'

'Not forgetting the thousands of dollars that went up in flames while we were fighting.' Barney pointed, drawing Jim's attention to the wrecked fire and, more important, the paper money that was now fuelling that fire.

Jim watched the money crisp, curl then burn.

'You'll talk your way into more money one day and besides, it was better to watch it burn than let Nixon get his hands on it.'

Barney chuckled, then roared with laughter. Jim joined in the laughter as they both tried to let good humour remove the memory of the last few minutes. When their laughter had died down the two men moved to seat themselves, a few chuckles still escaping their lips.

But then a new, echoing laugh sounded.

Jim froze, unsure for a moment what he'd heard, but the laughter sounded again and he swirled round to look away from the fire.

Three men were pacing into the firelight. Jim recognized two of them as being from the group who had tried to overcome them back on the trail. He glanced at his gun, but it was twenty yards away and all three men had already drawn their guns.

'Obliged that you made all that noise to tell us where you were,' the lead man said, 'or we might just have headed on by.'

CHAPTER 12

'Have you seen this before?' Sheriff Price asked, fingering the length of metal that hadn't been far from his hand since he'd found it last night.

Billy looked up from his cot to consider the gleaming object through the bars.

'Perhaps,' he murmured, then returned to staring at his feet.

Price gripped a bar with one hand and waved the metal with the other.

'Think!' he urged.

Billy must have caught Price's change of tone, for he swung his legs down from his cot and looked at the metal more closely.

'Orson used it to move those letter blocks into the right positions. He didn't trust me to do it, but he often held it. Is it important?'

'Was he holding it when he got shot? Did he drop it?' Price took a deep breath before he asked the question that had resonated in his mind since last night. 'Did you pick it up?'

Billy narrowed his eyes, then got to his feet and paced across the cell to face Price. He considered him, his head cocked to one side, sizing him up. Then he closed his eyes and kneaded his forehead, appearing as if he was concentrating. When he opened his eyes he shook his head.

'I could lie and say I heard someone behind me in the office and I was holding that, but I have to stick to the truth. That's what my pa said I should do, and I will.'

'But can you remember Orson holding it on the day he died?'

'Yeah.' Billy frowned, then returned to his cot where he sat and turned round to face Price. 'He was working on an important article so I kept out of his way.'

'What article?' Price asked, an inkling of an idea coming to him.

'I don't know, but I do know he was using that and I do know I wasn't holding a gun.'

'I believe you.'

'Enough to free me?'

'I'm not so sure about—'

'He will,' a clear voice uttered from the doorway behind him.

Price turned on his heel, his heart beating faster at the thought of being discovered discussing such a risky subject, but found that he faced Isaiah Jones.

'You were listening?' he asked, lost for anything else to say.

'To you and to everyone else in town. And I now

know what's going on in White Ridge.' Isaiah smiled. 'And what you're thinking is right. You should free Billy right away.'

'I can't,' Price murmured. 'I need Nixon's permission to do that.'

'Then get it,' Isaiah said. He paced into the law office, letting Price see that he had a roll of posters under his arm. 'I've heard that Jim McGuire and Barney Dale should arrive in White Ridge soon, one way or the other. Then the quest to bring the real killer to justice will begin.'

'But how can I prove anything? Knowing that Billy is innocent is one thing, proving who is guilty is another. There's no evidence, nothing to go on other than suspicions.'

Isaiah came across the office, then peeled off the outermost poster from beneath his arm. He held it out.

'Would it help if Orson Brown wrote out the name of his murderer before he died?'

'He didn't do that. I saw him die and he wasn't doing no writing.'

'I don't mean he revealed the name of the man who murdered him. I mean he was murdered because he revealed that name.'

Price took the offered paper and opened it out. Presented to him was a fragmented jumble of printed letters. Some formed themselves into completed words and some sense was probably in there if he were to stare at it hard enough, but to save time he looked up at Isaiah.

'Where? What is this?'

'It's the reason he died. For eight years Orson Brown supported Mayor Nixon, but his conscience plagued him. On the eve of the election campaign he planned to publish an article exposing everything Nixon had done.'

'I knew it!' Price cried, pleased that he'd already suspected that that was the case. 'Billy told me he was working on something important, something that had made him jumpy.'

'So he had to die. Afterwards, the text he'd put together got obliterated, but it looks like a jumble anyhow and whoever destroyed it wasn't careful enough to finish the job. When I printed off what remained, some of its original content survived.'

Isaiah pointed and with his help Price was able to make out words in a line of abbreviated text appearing about halfway down the page.

'*Funds*,' he read, '. . . something, then . . . *have then misapp . . . misappr. . . .*'

'Misappropriated.' Isaiah smiled when Price furrowed his brow. 'Stolen if you prefer.'

Now finding it easier to make sense of the jumble, Price carried on.

'*Town . . . eight years . . . fear and . . . and . . . murder . . . Overton . . . and Mayor Jake Nixon.*' Price received an encouraging nod from Isaiah and now that he'd worked out that Nixon's name was there he saw that parts of his name were all over the page. 'Have you worked out the whole story?'

'No, but I've worked out enough to decide it was an

article that would ruin Nixon.'

'And so he killed Orson, or had him killed?'

'I am just a candidate for mayor. You are the lawman. That is for you to work out.'

Price gulped. 'So what should I do?'

'I would have thought it was obvious. First, you need to collect the evidence of the original text from Orson's cupboard and bring it here for safekeeping. Then you need to decide whether it is significant enough to make an arrest. Then you need to make that arrest.' Isaiah slapped him on the shoulder. 'But whatever you do, I have every confidence in you.'

'And what will you be doing while I get myself killed?'

'I believe others should see this information and reach their own conclusions.' Isaiah patted the roll of paper beneath his arm. 'I ran off enough copies to post up everywhere around town.'

'A heap of trouble sure is heading our way,' Price murmured.

With that resigned comment he headed to the door. When he got there he stopped to take what he hoped would not be his last look around the office. Isaiah had the key to the cells and was approaching Billy's cell.

'You really going to free me?' Billy asked.

'Of course,' Isaiah said, putting the key in the lock. 'And while we wait for Sheriff Price to do his duty we can have ourselves a little talk.'

'About what?'

Isaiah threw open the cell door as Price left the office.

'I'd like to talk,' he said, 'about Jim McGuire.'

'So, Barney,' Jim demanded, 'when will you and your famous mouth start talking our way out this?'

Barney glared back at him. 'Be quiet or I'll only speak for myself and leave you here to get shot up.'

'Do that and I'll track you down and—'

'Be quiet!' a strident voice barked out.

One of their two captors came over to stand before them. He waited until they'd both quietened, then gestured at the other man to check their bonds. His rough tugging on their ropes removed most of their willingness to argue and once they'd been left alone they opted for sullen silence.

Daylight had now come and both men had spent an uncomfortable and largely sleepless night, trussed up at the wrists and ankles with heavy coils of rope. Jim had noted that the three men who had accosted them had taken part in the failed ambush further upriver.

During the night one of their number had left, but the reduction in the number of people guarding them gave Jim no comfort as he presumed he had gone in search of Pike. As the morning wore on, their captors' frequent glancing around and muttered conversations confirmed this.

The sun had poked above the ridge when their captors started acting in an animated manner while looking upriver. Jim tensed, hoping that if someone was coming it might distract them and let him escape. But one man kept an eye on them at all times while the other moved out of sight to shout out a barking cry.

130

The returning holler came from Pike and removed Jim's last shred of hope. He glanced at Barney who hunched further into himself as he awaited the inevitable.

When Pike came into view he dismounted, then took in the forlorn sight of the burnt-up pile of bills before he paced over to stand before them.

'You did well,' he said to their captors. 'For your trouble take any money that didn't get burnt.'

'Obliged. What do we do with them?'

Pike looked at each prisoner in turn and gave a sneering shrug.

'I have no use for either man. Kill them, then throw the bodies in the river.' Pike turned to leave, letting their guard pace in and draw his gun, confirming that there would be no change of heart.

Jim darted his gaze to the river, then up the ravine slope, hoping he might see some chance for a distraction, but saw nothing. He struggled, but his bonds were as tight as they had ever been, so he raised his chin, determined to die sitting as tall as he could.

Barney showed no such fortitude.

'Wait!' he screeched.

The guard ignored him and levelled his gun on him.

'Everyone, wait!' Barney called out again. 'You need to hear this.'

This did make the guard glance at Pike for instructions. Pike paced to a halt then slowly turned.

'All right,' he said. 'Tell me what I need to hear before you die.'

Barney took a deep breath, composing himself for what would be an important statement.

'I'm more valuable to you alive than dead,' he said.

'How?' Pike demanded in a clipped tone that showed he was in no mood to listen to any half-baked pleas for clemency or obvious delaying tactics.

'Killing me won't still any rumours, but if I'm alive I can tell everyone what I saw.' Barney widened his eyes. 'And that can be whatever Nixon tells me to say. There must be someone he wants to get rid of.'

Pike nodded slowly. 'That's an interesting idea. I'll think about it while we're disposing of Jim's body.'

'Don't,' Barney urged, as the guard turned his gun on to Jim. 'He's valuable too, but in a whole different way. He has money. That's why Sherman Donner wanted his backing, but I'm sure Nixon could have it instead.'

Jim sighed in exasperation. He'd lost count of the number of men he'd tracked down who, when they were staring down the barrel of his gun, had remembered they had a buried stash of money. It had never helped any of them and he didn't believe Pike was gullible enough to believe this tale either.

Sure enough Pike narrowed his eyes with scepticism, but there was also a suggestion from his lengthy pause before he replied that he might be seriously considering the bait.

'I find it odd,' he said, his tone sarcastic, 'that you came up with a reason why neither of you should die when you're sitting on the wrong end of a gun. I have my orders. You'll both die.'

'Don't!' Barney screeched, losing his calm manner for the second time. 'That's the problem for you, ain't it?'

'What problem?' Pike snapped.

'That you take orders. Men who only take orders are doomed to get nothing more than the pay their master gives them. All that ever happens to them is they end up dead like Hyde did. Men who can think, who can show they're more useful than the gun they wield, can achieve so much more.'

'Nixon likes people who follow orders.'

'Then follow them and never get anything from the set-up in White Ridge, until you end up dead and forgotten like Hyde.'

For long moments Pike considered Barney, then gave a nod.

'I'll take you two to Nixon and he can decide your fate.' He pointed a firm finger at Barney. 'But give me one moment's trouble and I'll risk following orders.'

'Much obliged.' Barney held out his hands. 'And cutting through these would show your good faith.'

As Pike snorted his breath and advanced a pace on Barney, Jim sighed in exasperation.

'Barney,' he urged from the corner of his mouth, 'be quiet.'

'I see no need,' Barney said, smiling at Pike. 'We've established we're on the same side. You can keep Jim tied up if you want but I'm no gunslinger. I'll be no trouble, no trouble at all.'

'You've been plenty all ready,' Pike grunted.

'Not as much as I will be when Nixon finds out that

you've mistreated a valuable ally. With Jim's money and my—'

'I ain't listening,' Pike said. He grabbed Barney's collar and yanked him to his feet.

'You should. If you want to become more than you are right now, you should learn to think about—'

'Be quiet!' Pike demanded, tugging Barney a few inches higher. 'I've never known anyone to talk so much for so little reason.'

'People have told me that I talk too much, I agree, but I prefer to say that I—'

An aggrieved roar tore from Pike's lips and with a round-armed slug he hammered Barney's jaw, sending him reeling. Barney came to a halt on his side, then tried to get to his feet, but Pike was already on him. He hoisted Barney up again and thumped him in the guts, making him fold. Then he yanked him upright and punched him a third time.

'Had enough?' Pike asked with his fist drawn back.

'I don't know why you're hitting me,' Barney whined. 'I was just trying to explain that—'

'Because,' Pike roared, punctuating every word with another punch that sent Barney stumbling backwards, 'you talk too damn much.'

His final punch sent Barney spinning into the saddlebags the guards had piled up, giving him a soft landing. Despite that he lay, gasping for breath, until Pike went over and kicked him in the side.

'Had enough?' he asked.

Barney made an obvious show of clamping his lips together while nodding.

'Then that lesson was worth giving,' Pike said. 'Any more talk from you and I'll batter you from here to White Ridge and let Nixon pick over whatever remains, understood?'

Pike waited until Barney gave another silent nod, then he left. The guard dragged Barney to his feet and marched him over to Jim. He threw him to the ground and the battered Barney could do nothing to stay his fall. He tumbled heavily against Jim and lay propped against him, moaning.

Jim waited until he was sure that Pike wouldn't change his mind and that the guards had returned to their steady patrol before he thanked Barney.

'Your mouth did well there,' he said.

'Yeah,' Barney murmured, wincing as he shifted position. 'I talked us out of trouble better than your gun would have done, didn't I?'

'I guess you did, but you have to learn when to be quiet.'

'Why? I did all right.'

Barney sat up straighter and the motion pushed something cold and metallic against Jim's wrist. Jim tensed then looked down to see that clutched in Barney's hands behind his back was a small knife, something he'd obviously purloined from the saddle-bags.

'Perhaps,' Jim said approvingly, 'you should carry on talking too much, after all.'

CHAPTER 13

Sheriff Price stopped at the back door of the newspaper office. Isaiah hadn't boarded up the office after he'd printed off the posters and Price slipped inside without difficulty.

He paced across the room to the cupboard where Orson Brown kept the block of incriminating text, but the door had been broken.

He looked on the floor then began rummaging, hoping he could find it, then stepped back to survey the scene.

'Is this what you're looking for?' a voice demanded from behind him.

Price swirled round to see Mayor Nixon standing in the doorway. Nixon glared at Price, then threw a tray of brass letters to the floor where they landed with a crash, scattering the remnants of Brown's article in all directions.

Despite the shock of Nixon's unexpected arrival Price was pleased he didn't feel as nervous as he'd thought he would be.

'I came here to collect that,' he said, 'but it seems you've destroyed it.'

Nixon pointed at the scattered letters. 'Why would this interest you?'

'Because it could be important evidence in proving who killed Orson Brown.'

Nixon tutted, then gestured behind him. Deputy Carter walked in to join him. Slowly both men came across the room to stand before Price.

'Now, Price,' Nixon said with steady menace, 'didn't I warn you about what would happen if you continued to pretend you were a lawman? Why haven't you heeded that warning?'

'Because I am a lawman.'

Nixon narrowed his eyes as he considered him, but Price met that gaze.

'You sound different today, Price,' Nixon said. He glanced at Carter, who uttered a surly warning grunt. 'It's almost as if you've got yourself a backbone. I don't like it.'

'I haven't changed. I'm still the man I was eight years ago when I was Sheriff Overton's deputy. I've just been behaving differently for a while, but no longer.'

The mention of Overton's name made Nixon snort his breath and when he spoke again all sign of his previous conversational demeanour had gone.

'You've gone too far this time, Price.'

Price smiled. 'The same as Martin Overton did, and Orson Brown, and Sherman Donner, and perhaps even the same as Ronald Malone, or did he really leave town like you claimed?'

Nixon's glare confirmed that his guess was probably correct.

'You've been useful to me, Price, so I'll make this easy for you. You'll get to die real quick. I'll even give you a choice of whether it happens here, or we take you out of town.'

Deputy Carter moved in, meaning to grab his arms but Price took a quick pace backwards and raised a hand.

'I take the third choice,' he said.

Carter followed him but Price grunted a quick order for him to desist.

'Let's hear it,' he said, 'and it'd better be good if you want to avoid unnecessary suffering.'

'My choice is I'll be the one giving the ultimatum. Either you'll leave town voluntarily or I'll arrest you and you'll provide me with a full confession.' Price watched Nixon chuckle. 'We've worked well together for a while and I owe you that.'

Nixon laughed aloud, prolonging his amusement until Carter joined him in heaping scorn on the idea.

'You are an odd man, Price, but I'm not leaving town and you're not arresting me.'

'Then I can't protect you.'

Nixon raised his hand, aiming to order Carter to seize Price, but then stilled his hand.

'Protect me from what?'

'From what is about to happen. You didn't destroy the evidence. There are hundreds of copies of Orson Brown's article around White Ridge already. If I don't leave here with you under arrest, they'll go up on every door and on every post and on every window in town faster than your hired guns can tear them down. You won't keep the truth from the townsfolk no longer. This is over for you.'

'You're bluffing,' Nixon roared, his face reddening with an all-consuming anger such as Price could imagine he'd had when he'd killed Sherman Donner. 'Nobody would help a worthless runt like you.'

'Yesterday you might have been right, but in the last few hours I've made several good and influential friends. So, what's it to be, Jake, a cell in my law office?' Price paced up to Nixon and put all the pent-up venom of the last eight years behind his demand. 'Or do I run your sorry hide out of town?'

'When do we make our move?' Barney asked.

Jim considered the approaching town from the back of the wagon on which they were being transported.

He'd used the knife that Barney had purloined to slice through most of his own ropes and Barney's but to maintain the illusion that they were held securely he'd not cut them all the way through. This ensured the tension still held him in a tightly bound manner, but just one flick of the wrist from the blade he'd tucked up his sleeve and he would be free.

Now he had to await his moment to act. He'd decided that trying to escape while out of town was doomed to failure when he had Barney to protect and they had nowhere to hide, but White Ridge was sure to present him with many opportunities.

As they trundled down the main thoroughfare, Jim

saw that the main road was almost deserted. Pike drew everyone to a halt outside the mayor's office, then called for everyone except for one guard, who remained on the back of the wagon, to join him in debating their next actions.

From the snippets of conversation that Jim overheard Pike wanted someone else to speak to Nixon first, to gauge how he would react to Pike's having disobeyed his order by bringing them to town. But that matter became irrelevant when on the other side of the road the door to the newspaper office was kicked open. Mayor Nixon and Deputy Carter emerged, closely followed by Sheriff Price.

In a line they headed down the boardwalk towards the law office. Curiously, although they all looked at the wagon, they didn't break their stride.

Jim tensed as Pike waved to draw Nixon's attention, judging that his moment to act was fast approaching.

'We need to talk,' Pike shouted when Nixon didn't acknowledge him.

This time Nixon glanced his way but he still continued walking along the boardwalk. His failure to approach made Pike cast bemused glances at the other men. Jim also wondered why he was ignoring them, and he couldn't help but notice that the sheriff was walking at the back, his posture suggesting he had the other two under arrest. Jim shook that thought away as being impossible.

'Mayor Nixon,' Pike persisted, 'this is important. I've brought Barney Dale and Jim McGuire back to town. They need to talk to you.'

Nixon came to a halt. He glanced over his shoulder at Sheriff Price who rubbed his chin before nodding. Then all three men turned to head towards them.

'Why have you brought those men here?' Nixon asked when he reached them, his voice sounding less authoritative than usual.

'They have something interesting to tell you. Perhaps we should go up to your office and talk about it.'

'I'm afraid not. Sheriff Price here has other ideas.'

'Price,' Pike snorted, 'has ideas?'

'Too many these days, but perhaps to save time, you should bring them all along to the law office and we'll talk about it there.'

Pike nodded and gestured for the guard to get Jim and Barney down from the wagon.

'Hey,' Price said, stepping up to Nixon, 'I didn't give permission for them to come.'

'Permission!' Nixon spluttered, his jaw grinding. Then with a huge roar he drew back his fist and delivered a backhanded slap to Price's face that sent him spinning to the dirt. 'I don't need permission from the likes of you to do anything.'

Nixon kicked Price in the side, making the prone lawman bleat with pain. Jim saw the redness of Nixon's face as the uncontrollable anger that Barney had told him about overcame him.

Jim reckoned this was the right time to act. He let the guard pull him to his feet and usher him to the back of the wagon. Then, while the guard dragged Barney up, Jim jerked his arm to shuffle the knife down into his hand.

141

'Time for me to act,' Barney said, leaning towards him. 'I'll do all the talking.'

'I prefer,' Jim said, 'for me do the talking this time.'

Jim swung the knife round in his grip, aiming to cut through the last of his bonds and free himself, but at that moment Barney nudged him.

'Don't. I've got the best. . . .' Barney trailed off as his movement jarred the knife from Jim's hand. It dropped, hit the edge of the wagon with a dull clatter, then fell to the ground.

'What the. . . ?' the guard murmured, his comment drawing Nixon's attention and stopping him from delivering a third kick to Price's prone form.

Jim lurched backwards, bundling the guard back a pace, then leapt down to the ground and dropped to his knees as he searched for the knife. He also tugged on his ropes but they held firm despite the deep cuts he'd made.

Up on the wagon Barney tried to make amends for his unfortunate action by pushing himself before the guard and stopping him leaping down on Jim, but those efforts wouldn't hold the guard back for more than a few seconds.

'Get him!' Nixon shouted, the order making two men move towards him, but none of them had managed a single pace before an explosion of gunfire tore out.

First the man on the wagon, then a second and third man went spinning to the ground, their backs holed.

While everyone flinched and ducked as they searched for where the shooting had come from, Jim saw the gun-toting and black-clad man standing in the

142

law office doorway: Isaiah Jones. He raised his gun again but by now Mayor Nixon had seen him too. While running behind the wagon, he delivered quick instructions.

Returning gunfire exploded around the door and shattered the window, making Isaiah jerk back inside. But the moment the first volley had ended he risked coming out again and returning fire, and this time he was joined by a second shooter who edged out into the broken window to fire.

Jim didn't see who it was, but he put that from his mind when he saw that their guards and the mayor had dived down behind the wagon. He looked up at Barney on the wagon and received an acknowledging nod. Then they gave up trying to find the knife and ran for the law office.

Price had also had the same idea but he was merely crawling towards it on all fours while, sprinting with their hands bound behind their backs, Jim and Barney pounded across the road.

'Hurry,' Isaiah shouted, moving out to lay down a covering round of gunfire, his action being supported by the second defender. This time Jim saw that Billy Jameson was doing the shooting.

Then he hurtled through the door, closely followed by Barney.

'A knife,' Jim demanded.

Getting his meaning Isaiah broke off to collect a knife from Price's desk. He cut through Jim's bonds. Then he pointed to the armoury and slapped Jim's shoulder.

When Jim had collected a gun he joined Billy at the

window and aimed gunfire at the wagon. He saw that Price was still crawling slowly towards them, but Nixon had focused his gunfire on the law office.

'Stop crawling and get in,' Isaiah shouted, but Price continued his slow way onwards.

'If you're helping Price, and the lawman defied Nixon by freeing Billy,' Jim said, looking at Billy and Isaiah in turn while smiling, 'then you sure have a great story to tell.'

'We do,' Billy grunted, his low tone not sounding pleased despite his freedom.

Jim cast him a bemused glance, then returned to helping Isaiah cover Price as he crawled up on to the boardwalk and came inside.

'What were you doing?' Isaiah demanded as Price shuffled past him. 'Nixon only kicked you.'

Price didn't reply until he'd crawled to his desk, where he squirmed round to sit with his back resting against it.

'He ignored me,' he murmured. 'I thought I'd made him respect me, but he just swatted me away like a fly, then couldn't even be bothered to kill me.'

Isaiah opened his mouth to respond, then shrugged and looked at Jim.

'You're right,' he said. 'There sure is a lot to explain, but it comes down to this: we're taking on Nixon. You with us?'

'Sure,' Jim said, deciding he didn't need to know anything else. He glanced at Billy. 'I never thought I'd get to work with you, but we'll get this done. Just keep your head down and follow my lead.'

'What do you care?' Billy grumbled.

Jim considered Billy's surly manner. He was used to his moods, but this appeared to be something more serious. The last time he'd seen him Billy had thought he was doomed to visit the gallows. Now he was free and yet he was looking at Jim with undisguised hatred.

'Not yet, Billy,' Isaiah said. 'We get ourselves out of this situation, then we settle the rest.'

'I want answers now,' Billy snapped.

Isaiah loosed off a couple of exploratory shots at the wagon, presumably to drag everyone's attention back to their immediate problem, but it had no effect on Billy, who glared at Jim from the opposite side of the window.

'To what?' Jim asked.

'To the question of who you are,' Billy muttered.

Jim shrugged, not understanding what Billy meant.

'I'm Jim McGuire,' he said.

'You ain't!' Billy snapped.

As Jim frowned, guessing where this might be leading, Isaiah placed a hand on Jim's shoulder.

'Billy and I have been talking,' he said.

'About what?' Jim said, turning to face Isaiah and seeing in his eyes the same kind of contempt that Billy was showing.

'About how you can't be Jim McGuire.'

'Why do you think that?' Jim murmured.

'Because,' Isaiah said, pointing at his own chest, 'I am Isaiah McGuire.'

145

CHAPTER 14

Over by the other window Barney glanced at Jim and frowned, then returned to looking outside, and this comment even made the self-pitying Sheriff Price look at them.

'You're Isaiah McGuire,' Jim murmured, 'from White Ridge?'

'I am,' Isaiah said with some relish.

'Is that the younger or the elder brother?'

'Elder.'

Jim nodded, making a reasonable guess as to what had happened. Isaiah appeared to be a few years older than the man he'd shot nine months ago, a man who, he now assumed, had been this man's brother.

'You were right earlier,' Jim said. 'We haven't got time to talk about this right now. The moment we have Nixon, I'll tell you the truth.'

'I know. I only saved your life so you and I can sort this out once and for all.'

Isaiah glared at him then swirled round to look around the side of the door, effectively dismissing the matter for now.

Jim looked at Billy hoping he'd give the same acknowledgement, that they'd postpone any discussion for later, but Billy wasn't as cool as Isaiah had been and returned a sneer that said he'd never want to hear any excuses.

With the contempt on either side of him making his ears burn, Jim watched the wagon. The gunfire had attracted attention throughout the town, but none of it was supportive. Windows had been shuttered up, people had fled from the road and, worse, the only people getting involved were several men making their way over to the wagon from the mayor's office to receive instructions from Nixon.

Jim counted ten men besides Nixon but, worse, he also noticed that Nixon was gesturing in other directions. This suggested that other, unseen, men were making a move to approach the law office from this side of the road.

'You reckon we'll get any help?' Jim asked.

'If it doesn't come soon it never will,' Isaiah said, his aggrieved tone showing he'd noticed the same problems as Jim had. 'I'd figured this town had lived under Nixon's thumb for too long and others would jump at the chance to help.'

'They might, but only if they think they can defeat him.'

'Then we need to make some headway and prove it's worth fighting back. Any ideas?'

Jim looked at Billy, but he just returned a contemptuous sneer that said he wouldn't talk to him even when his life was at stake. So he turned to the sheriff who was now rocking back and forth on the floor.

'What about you, Sheriff?' he asked.

Price took several seconds to acknowledge he'd heard him, then slowly looked up.

'He ignored me,' he murmured. 'He just batted me aside like a fly.'

'I gather you plucked up the courage to face up to Nixon, and that means you've got to see it through.'

Price looked at Isaiah, who smiled.

'You do it,' he said. 'I have confidence in you.'

'You had confidence in me before, but what good did it do me? I faced up to him. I arrested him. He showed respect for me and came along but he was just humouring me. He batted me aside. He just batted me aside.'

Isaiah and Jim glanced at each other silently, realizing that they'd get no help from him. Barney also shook his head.

'If you're looking to fight your way out of this,' he said, 'I won't be much use. But if you want me to talk my way out of this, I reckon I can oblige.'

'Talking won't keep the bullets away,' Isaiah said to a supportive grunt from Jim.

'I know, but it might stop them getting fired in the first place.'

Jim glanced outside at Nixon who was gesturing again, his urgent movements suggesting that whatever assault he was planning was imminent.

He shook his head. 'I can't let you get yourself killed on some foolish plan.'

'Agreed,' Isaiah said. So, with nothing else left to discuss, for several seconds they listened to feet scampering outside as Nixon's men got themselves into position for an assault.

Jim was preparing himself to begin shooting when Sheriff Price spoke up, and for the first time since he'd crawled into the law office his voice sounded confident.

'Barney is right with one small proviso,' he said. He got to his feet, making everyone in the room look at him. He stood with a straight back and a confidence in his eye that hadn't been there a few moments earlier. 'Nixon won't listen to Barney, but he will listen to me.'

Two minutes later Sheriff Price stood before the door, his gun drawn but held lowered and his other hand clamped firmly on Barney's shoulder. When he received Isaiah's cue he raised his gun and fired twice into the ceiling. Then he counted to ten before kicking open the door to stand framed in the doorway. The other three men inside kept themselves back from the doorway and windows to avoid being seen.

'Don't shoot,' Price shouted. 'I'm bringing 'em out.'

Price pushed Barney outside and followed him. When he'd moved out of Jim's sight Jim crawled along the floor to the window and risked peering through a corner of the broken pane. Billy was still standing close to him but out of sight, and Isaiah had taken up a position beside the other window.

Jim tried to catch Billy's eye, hoping that maybe the formulation of this plan to defeat Nixon might have cheered him, but Billy wouldn't look at him.

Outside, Price and Barney moved into view to reach the edge of the boardwalk, then stepped into the road, so Jim consoled himself with the thought that they'd got further than he'd thought they would.

'What're you doing, Price?' Nixon demanded from behind the wagon.

'I got 'em,' Price shouted. 'I got 'em all. Everything's fine and it's all down to me.'

Several men emerged from behind the wagon and the glances that Price cast around told Jim where the other men were hiding.

'I ain't a fool, Price. You tried to arrest me earlier. Stop where you are.'

Price kept walking. 'You don't order me around no more, Jake. I take care of the law in White Ridge. I took care of Isaiah Jones and Jim McGuire and now I've got this one under arrest. He says he's got an interesting story to tell.'

'I ain't interested in hearing it.'

'And to tell you the truth, neither am I.' Price stopped and threw Barney to his knees. 'That man only speaks in lies. His word means nothing, but that's my decision to make, ain't it, Nixon?'

With a glance at the men around him, Nixon came out from behind the wagon.

In the law office, Jim ducked down, then gestured to Isaiah.

'It's working,' he whispered. 'I don't believe it but he's got Nixon interested enough to come out into the open.'

'Just give the word and we go for 'em,' Isaiah said.

Jim nodded then returned to watching what was happening outside, where Nixon was still walking towards Price. He stopped ten paces away from the sheriff, with four men flanking him.

'What are you trying to tell me, Price? That I should let you live? That I should let you be a real lawman?'

'That's all this was about: respect. Respect me and I'll respect you.'

'I never wanted respect from the likes of you.' Nixon looked over to the side. 'Carter, get into the law office and check whether this fool really did what he said he did.'

In the office Jim tensed, accepting that Price's plan would probably not work now, but hoping the element of surprise would earn them an advantage. Barney caught on to the urgency of the situation and jumped to his feet.

'Let me speak, Mayor,' he said, talking quickly as he edged towards Nixon. 'I didn't see nothing back in your office when I was stealing your money, but I sure can—'

'Be quiet! I'm only interested in whether this fool can be trusted.'

'That's what I want to talk to you about. I—'

'Enough!' Nixon shouted, advancing on Barney with a hand raised, making Barney cringe away.

At that moment Jim saw a shadow fall across the window. He stayed still as Deputy Carter darted his head around, looking through the broken window into the dark office.

'Can't see nobody in there,' he called out.

'I threw them in a cell,' Price shouted back.

Carter walked past the window, moving towards the door, temporarily blocking Jim's view of the road where Nixon walked past the cringing Barney to stand before Price.

'Perhaps,' he said as inside the office Jim and Isaiah tensed, awaiting their imminent discovery, 'you might be getting that respect you wanted.'

'Respect,' Price said. 'That is *all* I ever wanted.'

Price then raised his gun and shot Mayor Nixon in the stomach, making him fold and stagger forward a pace. A hail of bullets tore out from Nixon's men, sending Price tumbling backwards but not before he'd planted another bullet in Nixon.

Then Carter swung the door open and took Jim's thoughts away from what was happening in the road.

Isaiah leapt to the side to blast lead through the door. A pained cry sounded as Isaiah vaulted the shot Deputy Carter in the doorway to emerge on to the boardwalk. Jim followed him.

'Stay here,' he shouted at Billy, but didn't stay to check whether Billy had followed his instructions.

He emerged outside to confirm that the men he'd thought were moving in on either side were close, but the shooting in the road had distracted them. Isaiah and Jim made them pay with rapid spurts of gunfire.

Without consulting each other Isaiah went left and Jim went right, shooting on the run.

Five men were on Jim's side and he took out three with his first burst of gunfire, then went to his knees, reloading with a dexterity that had saved his life many times before. By the time he'd reloaded the surviving men had got their wits about them. Jim put that from his mind and ran for the hitching rail.

Splinters flew from the post and rail as Jim vaulted it, his rapid motion saving him from a shot that whined past his shoulder. When he landed he went to one knee and jerked up his gun, sighting the nearest man in an instant and blasting him in the chest. Then he swung his red-hot gun to the side to take out the remaining standing man on his side.

He glanced along and up the buildings on his side of the road to confirm that nobody was attempting to outflank him, and turned. Isaiah had already shot the four men who had been approaching from his side and was now running for the wagon where Price was lying, holed mortally, but so was Nixon.

The lack of a leader had confused the surviving men and they were looking around for instructions, some even running for safety, their indecision having let Barney roll into cover beneath the wagon.

'Get 'em!' Pike's strident voice barked out from behind the wagon. The order stopped several men in their tracks. Then as one they turned to face the advancing Jim and Isaiah.

A gunshot rang out then a second, sending two men reeling. Jim noticed that Isaiah hadn't been the one who had fired. The gunfire had come from behind.

'Nice shooting, Billy,' he murmured to himself.

A third shot tore into another hired gun and that

left just Pike and three others. Isaiah took care of one of them before the rest scurried into hiding behind the wagon. Then he threw himself to the ground to lie flat and directed his gun towards the wagon. Jim joined him.

From there he could see three sets of legs of the men who had crouched behind the wagon and without compunction Isaiah tore lead across those legs. One man fell to the side, letting Jim plant a bullet in his chest and a second went hopping out from behind the wagon whereupon Isaiah and Billy combined to send him reeling.

Pike, though, had the sense to roll over into the wagon where he lay flat and out of sight. For long moments they waited for him to show himself, but when he didn't Jim risked casting his gaze across at the devastation in the road. As far as he could tell Pike was their only opposition, but he was also the most formidable of Nixon's crew.

With hand signals he debated their next move with Isaiah, getting confirmation that Isaiah would cover Jim while he got closer to the wagon. So Jim got to his feet, then doubled over, made his quick and snaking way over to the wagon.

He stopped five feet from the backboard, where he ran his gaze over the wood, looking for a gap in the boards and a sight of his quarry.

Pike stayed down and out of sight, forcing Jim to pace slowly around the wagon. Jim glanced at Barney, who was lying beneath the front of the wagon and raised his eyebrows. Barney pointed towards the back but then roved his finger from side to side saying he wasn't sure of Pike's exact position.

With each sideways pace Jim raised his head slightly. More of the wagon came into view, letting him see the seat. He concluded that Pike must be lying flat. He also saw that there were numerous knotholes along the back boards. . . .

He dived to the ground, his action saving him from the slug that spewed from the gun barrel poking through one knothole. Jim rolled, scrambling himself along towards the wagon to come up underneath it.

As Pike's ill-aimed shot had let him judge where he was lying, on his back he fired upwards then twice more, each shot two feet apart. The third shot hit its target, making Pike grunt in pain and jerk away, but that only put him into Isaiah's view.

Twin shots rang out making Pike clatter to the base of the wagon. He rolled over the side to come to a halt on his back in an explosion of dust beside the wagon. He lay for a moment, then raised his gun towards Jim, but Jim had already aimed at him.

'Like Barney tried to tell you,' Jim said. 'Men like you just get to die and be forgotten.'

He fired, holing Pike's forehead. Then Jim looked at Barney and raised his eyebrows.

'Glad something I said stuck in your mind,' Barney said.

'It sure did,' Jim said, and swung his gun into his holster. 'But now that this is over, take some advice. Get yourself a gun before you find a problem that mouth of yours can't talk its way out of.'

Barney shook his head, so Jim rolled out from under the wagon. He stood, brushed the dust from his knees and found that there was only one man standing in the road: Isaiah Jones, also known as Isaiah McGuire.

Jim started to thank him for his help, but the words died on his lips. Isaiah had adopted the posture of a gunslinger, his legs splayed apart and his hand dangling beside his holster.

'We've dealt with Nixon,' Isaiah said, 'so now, like I promised, you'll tell me why you call yourself Jim McGuire. Then I'll kill you.'

CHAPTER 15

'I used to be fast,' Jim said, letting his hand drift towards his holster. 'I reckon I still am. If I go for my gun, I'll kill you and I don't want that to happen.'

'I'll take that chance. Speak, then die.'

Jim shrugged. 'If you're that determined, I won't draw. I've got no reason to kill you, and the truth is there was nothing personal between me and Jim McGuire . . . your brother, either. I was a manhunter and I'd been hired to kill Blaine Jameson, Billy's father. Your brother just got in the way.'

'You killed Billy's father! What kind of twisted animal are you?'

'The kind who realized he'd made a mistake. The kind who's spent the last nine months trying to make amends. The kind who risked his life to save Billy from the gallows.'

Isaiah sneered. 'To ease your conscience.'

'Sure, but that doesn't change the good I've done. Once you've killed a man you can't change what's happened. You can only make things right from then on. That's what I've been trying to do.'

'Is that all the excuses you're going to give me?'

'Yup.' Jim raised his hand away from his holster. 'I've got nothing else to say so you might as well kill me, but it won't bring back your brother and then you'll have to be the one who tries to do what's right for Billy.'

'Is that your way of pleading for your life?'

'Nope, just making a request of the kind Billy's father made before I killed him. Try to do the best for young Billy. Give him as good a start in life as you can.'

'I'll do that.' Isaiah narrowed his eyes. 'But I'd appreciate a word of regret from you first.'

'I could give it, but the man who killed Jim McGuire was a different man from the one standing before you. That man was a cold-blooded killer. This man thought he was good enough to wear the name Jim McGuire.'

Isaiah looked around, taking in the townsfolk emerging to look at Nixon's dead body. Excited chatter was building up and people were already laughing and smiling, suggesting that nobody would complain about the devastation that had been brought about.

'If I let you live,' Isaiah said, lowering his voice as his hand moved away from his holster, 'what will you do?'

'Try to explain myself to Billy, try to help him if he wants that help.'

Isaiah looked over his shoulder to see that Billy was edging his way out of the law office. The kid was watching them, his brow furrowed and confused. Isaiah relaxed.

'Don't tell him the truth,' he said, 'yet. Wait until

158

he's old enough to handle it.'

'He knows too much already.'

'Not *too* much. I can still tell him a story to explain what happened.' Isaiah offered a brief smile. 'Can't I, Brother?'

Jim returned that smile. 'You can. I've always trusted my elder brother.'

'And,' Barney said, stepping up to join them, 'if neither of you can spin a tale to keep Billy happy, I'm sure I can do it.'

'I'm sure you can,' Jim said ruefully.

'But remember this,' Isaiah said, 'I ain't that taken with you yet, so I intend to stay in White Ridge. If I see you aren't doing the right thing by Billy. . . .'

'I know.' Jim moved round to stand beside him so that they could greet the approaching Billy together. 'But if you're staying, does that mean you're still standing for mayor?'

'I reckon White Ridge would welcome having an honest mayor for a change.' Isaiah glanced at Jim. 'And a worthwhile lawman, if you're interested.'

'That's an . . .' Jim trailed off as Billy stomped to a halt before them.

'Now tell me everything,' Billy demanded, settling his stance. 'Who are you? What happened to my pa?'

'I've already told you everything,' Jim said in a low and reasonable voice. 'I'm Jim McGuire and I had some trouble, now resolved, with my elder brother. There's nothing for you to know about your pa that I haven't already told you a hundred times.'

'I don't understand.' Billy looked at Isaiah, who was

159

smiling, then at Barney, but when Barney started to open his mouth to comment, Jim paced forward and looped an arm around Billy's shoulders. He walked him away from the wagon.

'But I do have something important to tell you. I've finally found the right job for you, one that would have made your pa proud, one you've proved you're ideally suited for, and one where your boss will never fire you.'

'What's that?' Billy murmured, some of his truculence fading away.

'I'm to be White Ridge's new sheriff,' Jim said. 'How would you like to be my deputy?'